WOLF DESIRED

ENSNARED BY THE PACK: BOOK 3

TESSA COLE

Gryphon's Gate Publishing

Wolf Desired

Gryphon's Gate Publishing
550 King St. N.
PO Box 42088 Conestoga
Waterloo, ON
N2L 6K5

Print ISBN: 978-1-990587-12-2

AUDREY

BLAZING AGONY TORE AT MY BODY, RIPPING INTO MY CELLS, digging into my essence, and igniting my soul. Everything was on fire and every muscle had contracted. I was frozen in place with one hand gripping the side of the death god's altar, the other pressed on top of the altar — my fingers brushing Knox's — and my head thrown back with a scream I couldn't release.

I tried to breathe but couldn't. Tried to move, to think, to do anything to relieve the pressure and the inferno consuming me, but I was stuck.

Panic squeezed even tighter around my chest, an all-consuming terror that I'd made a horrible mistake. Not because I shouldn't have been trying to break my accidental mating bond with Knox, but because the spell we'd hoped would break the unbreakable was going to burn me up and leave nothing behind. Even if somehow my body survived, I'd be a shell, my soul completely devoured.

The fire tightened around my heart, ripping at the magic binding me to Knox. It heaved the bond from my chest, wrenching me forward, stretching, tearing, straining.

Tears streamed down my cheeks, and I squeezed my eyes shut, praying for it to be over, to finally be free.

Then the fire exploded, and the force yanked my soul out of my body determined to tear it apart before slamming it back into my chest. The impact knocked me over, suddenly releasing all my muscles, and I collapsed on the smooth floor of the death god's temple.

Bishop rushed to my side and gathered me in his arms, cradling me against his chest and wiping the tears from my cheeks.

"It's okay," he murmured. "I've got you. I've got you."

On the other side of the altar, Knox groaned. He hadn't been thrown back and had collapsed on top of the coffin-sized stone slab. The weak light filtering through the hole in the domed ceiling caught in the green flecks in his eyes.

They were so much like Bishop's and yet so different. They mesmerized me, drawing me in, stealing my breath, and connecting with that messed up something inside me that said he was mine.

"Fuck," he snarled, and the icy hollowness of his rejection crashed over me, consuming the painful, fiery remnants of the spell.

Oh, God. The frozen emptiness was even stronger than before, and I didn't know if that meant our mating bond was stronger or just his determination to get rid of me.

"Shit," Cyrus hissed, laying a hand on Knox's shoulder. "It didn't work, did it?"

"No." Knox batted Cyrus's hand away, shoved past him, and stormed out of the temple.

My throat tightened and a tear I didn't want to cry rolled down my cheek.

It hadn't worked.

We were stuck together.

Forever.

Or at least until one of us died, and I had a horrible feeling Knox would rather take his chances on going insane when I died than spend the rest of his life with me.

A sob tightened my throat and I buried my face against Bishop's shoulder, fighting to keep it in.

I could do this. I could live with this.

Knox and I would have to seal our bond before it drove both of us crazy, but then I could convince him that I didn't expect him to behave like my mate. I could find a room to rent in Stonehaven and spend a quiet life cleaning houses or something.

It wouldn't be so bad.

Except my soul wept at the thought. It didn't want to be without Knox. He was my mate. We belonged together.

And he doesn't want me. Never did. Never will.

That was the cold hard truth I was going to have to live with.

"It's okay," Bishop murmured, stroking my hair and holding me tight. "We'll get back to Stonehaven and see if Whil can transfer the bond to me."

Right. Plan B. All wasn't lost. We just needed to withstand the compulsion of the bond to seal it for another nine days.

A roar echoed down the narrow passage, the only way into the enormous chamber, and a shock of ferocious fury swept through the icy hollowness.

Oh, shit. He wasn't going to wait for plan B. He was going to kill me. Now.

My gaze slid to the altar.

Would he think he'd be able to avoid the side-effects of losing his mate if he sacrificed me to the death god? Would Cyrus and Bishop let him?

A shiver swept through me. I'd already had one supposed mate try to sacrifice me and I'd barely escaped with my life. I doubted I'd be so lucky a second time. Especially since Knox was more powerful than Royce and Sterling.

I shifted my attention to Bishop, looking up at him through my lashes. He was so beautiful, his features sculpted, a dusting of dark stubble along his jaw, and warm brown eyes that could capture my soul.

He'd been kind to me from the start, had vowed to

court me and make me his mate even if I was also mated to Knox. He wouldn't let him sacrifice me.

But would he be strong enough to protect me from his brother? From both his brothers?

Without a doubt, if Cyrus had to pick a side, he'd pick Knox's. He'd already made his priorities clear. His pack and family were first. Always first. And I was neither.

Bishop leaned back and met my gaze, his expression filled with so much concern it made my heart break and another tear rolled down my cheek.

No one had ever looked at me like that, like I mattered and I wasn't a burden even though I was. I'd yearned for someone to care for me like that all my life, and now it seemed I'd found someone just when everything was completely fucked up.

"Can you walk?" he asked, his voice soft as if he were afraid speaking too loudly would scare me.

I nodded even though I wasn't sure if my legs could hold me and reluctantly eased away from his embrace.

Knox roared again and a hint of alpha power squeezed around my chest. Bishop's attention jerked toward the passage, his body tensing, and an icy fear shivered down my spine.

Was Knox coming back? Was Bishop going to be forced to pick between me and his brother?

My throat tightened and more tears burned my eyes.

There was no contest. Knox was his twin, the other half of his human soul. It didn't matter how Bishop looked at me. A look was just a look. It didn't mean anything.

Cyrus marched back into the chamber and grabbed all three of our packs. "We need to go. I don't want to be on the death god's land when night falls. Carry her if she can't walk."

Then he marched back out. He hadn't even glanced my way and that only made the sinking feeling in my stomach grow. Some of Merrick's betas hadn't been able to look at me, either. They'd pretended I hadn't existed and that somehow absolved them of any responsibility for the child they knew their alpha was treating like a slave and abusing.

I sucked in a ragged breath, trying to steady my nerves. If we were leaving, Knox wasn't planning to sacrifice me. Which meant I might be the person no one wanted, but my life wasn't in immediate danger.

It was sad that that was my best situation... and that I'd have to be on guard for Knox or Cyrus to change their minds.

I sucked in another, steadier breath, and gathered the tattered remains of my determination. Bishop had a plan B and my heat was over. I could resist having sex with Knox for another nine days. It might only be eight if I could convince the guys to push our pace.

I could do this.

I'd already made it this far. I'd survived a man-eating monster. This unwanted mating bond was nothing.

And maybe if I kept telling myself that, I'd believe it.

"So," Bishop asked. "Am I carrying you?" A soft smile tugged at his lips as if he already knew my answer.

"No." I shoved up to my feet. My body was achy on a bone-deep level, but I couldn't have expected to go through that spell without some aftereffects.

I just needed to walk it off, perhaps get a night's sleep, and I'd be back to the way I was before. The way I'd felt yesterday morning when I'd woken boneless and satiated in bed with Bishop.

The memory of having sex with him shivered through me and I clung to the sensation. Feeling a little turned on was better than the icy hollowness any day. And now the sensation wasn't out of control. It was a low, sensual ache, burning at the edge of my senses. A memory that I could draw on to make myself feel better.

"Let's go," I told him.

So, plan A hadn't worked, plan B was a long shot, and I had no idea what plan C was... if there even was a plan C. But I hadn't given up during the years of suffering with Merrick and Sterling, and I wouldn't give up now.

AUDREY

I STRODE OUT OF THE TEMPLE, AN ENORMOUS, SHAPELESS, windowless mound in the middle of flat, barren nothingness as far as the eye could see.

Knox paced about fifty feet away, his movement jerky, anger radiating off him. It shocked me that he was still in human form. I would have thought he'd have shifted before even getting out of the temple's dark passageway given that he preferred his wolf form over his human one.

Without a word, Cyrus handed one of the packs to Bishop and started marching south. Knox took that as permission to leave — I wasn't sure why he'd even stuck around — and, with a jerk of Cyrus's chin, Bishop hurried to catch up with his twin.

Swell. Just what I needed. Left with the brother who thought I couldn't do anything and that I was going to be a burden to his family and pack for the rest of my life.

I'd been trying to prove this whole walk here that I

wouldn't hold him or anyone back. I might not know anything, but I'd been, and still was, determined to not complain and keep up.

I'd thought from our conversation last night where he seemed to have respected my desire to live independently that he was softening up to me. But now, from the tension in his shoulders and back, I guess I'd been wrong.

"I can carry my own pack," I said, even as the ache in my body grew, complaining about our current pace.

His gaze slid to mine, his moss green eyes edged with his wolf's darkness, his expression hard and unreadable even as it sent a shiver of desire teasing down my spine. Was he furious like Knox?

I huffed at myself. Of course he was.

He'd been angry at me since we'd left Stonehaven and now all hope of getting rid of the weakling was gone. Even plan B meant I was still part of the family... of course, if Bishop intended to court me regardless of the spell's outcome, I'd still end up part of the family.

My toe caught on an uneven crack in the almost completely flat ground, and I staggered two steps before catching my balance.

Cyrus raised one eyebrow as if he couldn't believe I'd actually found something to trip on.

"Walk for an hour without tripping. Then you can get your pack back." He jerked his attention back to Knox and Bishop, who were now at least a hundred feet ahead of us.

Fine. I could do that.

"We all knew the spell was a long shot," he said a few minutes later, his gaze still straight ahead. "Bishop's plan B has even worse odds."

"It might be possible," I insisted even though I knew Cyrus was right.

Still, the fae sorcerers that had helped the Angelic Defense defeat Michael had been incredibly powerful. Whil had said she wasn't magically strong, but that didn't mean she wouldn't be able to do it. I had no idea what was considered a "weak" sorcerer. She probably had more power in her baby finger than I did in my entire body.

"Anything is possible." Cyrus glanced at me, his expression soft and sad.

God, he was just as beautiful as his brothers except in a more rugged, edgy way, and seeing him look at me like that, like he actually cared, made my pulse stutter.

Had I been wrong about him? I'd assumed everything I did pissed him off, but maybe that wasn't true and he just wasn't great at showing his feelings.

Then his expression hardened, his walls returning, and he faced forward again. "But you're smart enough to know moving a mating bond isn't probable," he added.

"I don't have any other option. Knox doesn't want me." The icy hollowness in my chest surged and I fought to push it back.

"Both of you are going to have to accept the reality of your situation," he said, the angry edge returning to his voice. "The sooner you do, the better for Knox."

And there it was. The reminder that Knox was, and always would be, Cyrus's first priority.

"So, I just have to accept that I'm going to spend the rest of my life in a loveless mating because that's what's best for Knox, for the pack? You're just as bad as my old pack."

My toe caught on another crack and I stumbled again.

This time I couldn't catch my balance and careened forward, but Cyrus caught me before I could smash my knees on the hard ground and yanked me against his body.

My hands slid across his broad, sculpted chest, and his powerful arms surrounded me. His deep earthy scent wrapped around me like a blanket, comforting and warm until the warmth began to grow.

The last time I'd been this close to Cyrus, we'd been in Stonehaven and he'd been yelling at me for risking my life. And he'd been naked.

My breath hitched. I knew what all that bulky muscle looked like, and now I was getting a moment to know what it felt like to be wrapped in it.

The heat dropped to my core and turned the soft, achy memory of having sex with Bishop into something deeper and stronger.

"Are you saying you're not open to multiple mates?" he asked, his voice gruff. "Will you refuse Bishop? If Whil can't transfer the bond, you and Knox are stuck together, but that doesn't mean that has to be everything in your life."

I tipped my head to look up at him, and his gaze flickered to my lips before jumping back to my eyes.

"And you'd accept that?" I breathed, my lips tingling with the need for him to kiss me. "The weakest shifter in existence mated to both of your brothers?"

He cupped my cheek with his large palm. "I think we've already established that you're not the weakest. You've killed a grimalkin—"

"By accident," I reminded him.

"You've stood your ground against them twice, and you've walked until your feet bled on the chance you could set my brother free. Those are not the actions of a weak shifter." He huffed a soft laugh. "A foolish one, maybe, but not weak."

I dropped my gaze, unable to keep looking him in the eyes. I didn't know what to do with words like that. I'd never been good enough or strong enough or anything enough, and just hearing that maybe I was, that maybe Cyrus saw me as something more than a weakling, made my insides squirm.

"I can't shift," I murmured. "My children might have the same curse I have." And they might have the same problem. Unlike the rest of my pack whose wolf had awoken on the summer solstice after their eighteenth birthday, mine was still asleep and probably always would be... if I even had a wolf half to my soul.

"Bishop doesn't care." Cyrus brushed a stray lock of my dirty blond hair away from my eyes then hooked his thumb under my chin, forcing me to meet his gaze again. "He's never courted a woman before—"

"I find that hard to believe." From everything I'd seen, Bishop had left a trail of broken hearts behind him.

"Oh, he's dated and flirted, but his wolf was never interested. Not until you." His eyes dipped back to my mouth, and my pulse picked up, my body yearning for his lips on mine.

I leaned into him and breathed in his scent, my pulse pounding in my ears. Cyrus had never shown any interest in me before, and while a tiny voice in the back of my mind was screaming that this was wrong, this was how my body responded when I was in heat, the rest of me didn't care. He was stunning and powerful, and he'd never be mine, but oh how my body wanted a taste of what it would be like.

Then the muscles in his jaw flexed, and he slid both hands to my shoulders and took a large step back.

The sudden separation sent chills rushing over me, and not just because I'd lost his body heat. He was rejecting me. He'd had a moment of weakness, a moment my now throbbing core desperately wanted, and realized it was a mistake.

"You're not without options, Audrey," he said, his voice gruff. "Just remember that when Whil can't free you from Knox." He turned back toward Knox and Bishop, who were even farther ahead of us. "Come on. We're falling behind."

"Right." I fought to swallow my disappointment,

confused about why I'd reacted so strongly to him, and hurried to catch up.

He set an even faster pace than before and I struggled to keep up. I was already achy — sore *and* turned on — and the longer I walked, the achier I became. I wasn't walking off the side effects of the spell, and now I couldn't stop staring at Cyrus's ass or his broad, powerful shoulders easily carrying the packs... one of which I should have been carrying.

On top of that, the chill in the air that had deepened the closer we'd gotten to the temple didn't warm up the farther we went away. Even with the sun still sitting high in the sky and blazing down on us, I shivered, which didn't help with the achy muscles.

The path grew rockier and scraggly weeds and bushes started to dot the landscape. Cyrus was hot enough that I could see sweat darkening the back of his shirt every time one of the packs shifted, which made me think of my hands sliding over his slick skin, those bulky muscles flexing as he drove into me.

Fuck. I squeezed my eyes shut. What was wrong with me? Why was I thinking about sex with Cyrus when I could be remembering sex with Bishop?

My thoughts lurched to the previous night and how Bishop's sleeker body had looked as he pushed oh-so-carefully inside me—

I stumbled over the uneven ground, the ache in my body sinking deep into my hips and back, making each step harder and harder.

A whisper of a breeze swept over us, rattling the dead stalks of grass, catching in strands that had fallen out of Cyrus's braid, and making my teeth chatter.

Hugging myself, I fought to control my trembling, but that upset my balance and I stumbled again, bashing my knee against a rocky outcropping.

Shit.

I swallowed back my curse, not wanting to alert Cyrus that I still couldn't walk a straight line without a pack, and limped forward. The injury wasn't bad, but the impact had jarred up my entire body, pointing out every achy muscle and joint.

Rocky landscape meant we were getting closer to the abandoned village where we were going to spend the night.

I just needed to push a little farther, and then I could take a break because I wholeheartedly agreed with Cyrus. I didn't want to be caught on the death god's lands after dark.

The guys had warned me about this realm's spirits that were manifestations of a god or goddess's power, and I didn't want to encounter any that belonged to a death god.

But as I raised my gaze to see where we were — and how far ahead Cyrus was — the world lurched to the side, and I bumped my hip against another outcropping.

Staggering, I clutched at the rib-high protrusion to catch my balance. The rock beneath my hand swam in and out of focus, darkening and lightening as if clouds were rapidly passing overhead even though there hadn't been a cloud in the sky.

The world lurched again despite not even looking up, and my knees trembled, threatening to drop me to the ground.

Something wasn't right and I wasn't going to be able to tough it out until we made camp. And even if I could tough it out, Cyrus had been pissed because I hadn't told him that my feet had been sore, bleeding messes for days. He hadn't yelled at me during our conversation about accepting my bond and I really wanted to keep it that way.

I looked up, gritting my teeth against my lurching, darkening vision. He was even farther away than before, but I didn't know if he really was or if that was tunnel vision.

"Cyrus," I gasped, my voice ringing in my ears. "I—"

My core clenched hard and a wave of clawing, desperate need stole my breath along with my vision. I sagged to the ground, my legs unable to hold me, the world so dim it felt like the dead of night. Shivers wracked my body. The trembling exacerbated my feverish aching and the painful throbbing in my core.

I needed sex.

I needed I needed I needed.

I couldn't think of anything else and my need was going to consume me if I didn't satisfy it.

CYRUS

My wolf heaved against my control and I fought to hold him back as I marched after Knox and Bishop.

What the fuck was wrong with me? I'd had Audrey in my arms and all I could think about was kissing her. She was hurt and scared, the spell she'd put her faith in had failed — and it looked like it had been painful — and I was thinking about what her lips would feel like and taste like.

I'd been trying to do the right thing and convince her to accept Knox as her mate, and then she'd tripped and I'd lost my fucking mind.

Of course, it wasn't really Audrey who needed to accept the mating bond, but she was the one who was going to get hurt the most. She needed to be prepared and understand that it wasn't the end of her world. Because the thought of her continuing to suffer made my wolf howl and threaten to take over.

I didn't want Knox to suffer, either, but no one, not even Bishop, was going to be able to convince him to accept his fate.

Unfortunately, the stubborn asshole's inner battle was tearing a rift between him and his animal half, and I feared when I released the collar containing his wolf, the beast would take over and we'd lose him again. This time permanently.

It had taken everything I had to keep the collar intact when the spell had failed and the pressure of being inside the temple had become too much for my brother.

Next time, I might not get so lucky.

And without a doubt, there'd be a next time before we decided it was safe to let his wolf loose.

Which was why I'd sent Bishop to walk with him. Bishop could help calm him down as well as add another layer of compulsion to the collar which would hopefully keep Knox contained until we got back to Stonehaven and attempted Bishop's next-to-impossible plan B.

But that had left me with shivering, too-pale, wide-eyed Audrey and the need to say something.

I wasn't good at placating or telling sweet lies to make someone feel better. That was Bishop's job. I was the practical brother. I saw problems and addressed them, and Audrey refusing to accept the inevitable was a problem that could shatter her burgeoning confidence.

If she embraced it, she could plan for it. The emotional blow wouldn't be so hard, and she wouldn't have to figure out her next steps while caught in an emotional whirlwind. Steps like where she lived and what she wanted to do with her life.

Just because she and Knox were mated didn't mean they had to live together, at least not until they grew more comfortable in the bond and it compelled them closer.

But I had a feeling she wouldn't think of that. Certainly not while she believed her life had been permanently turned upside down. I could even see her thinking that she belonged to Knox since power and strength had played a strong role in her old life. I'd gotten the impression that for her, the powerful owned the weak, and the weak had no say.

And then she'd tripped and every protective instinct I'd had surged along with my wolf's determination that she was mine.

For fuck's sake. I couldn't be her mate. No matter what my wolf wanted.

She couldn't ever be mine. I had responsibilities to my pack and they wouldn't see Audrey the way I did, wouldn't see the determined, resilient beautiful woman I'd caught glimpses of on our journey here. They'd constantly question and challenge her, and she'd retreat back into her shell.

No. I wouldn't do that to her.

If she could accept the idea of multiple mates, Bishop would love and support her in ways neither Knox nor I could. Knowing he cared for her and was more than capable of protecting her would have to be enough.

I swallowed back a growl and rolled my shoulders,

trying to loosen the tension in my body. I needed my wolf to calm the fuck down. He'd been going insane since the spell had ripped through her body, her expression locked in agony, and he hadn't been able to do anything.

Nothing was going to happen with Audrey. Not now. Not ever.

Audrey gasped my name, her voice barely audible and strained, and the sound jerked me from my whirling thoughts.

I wrenched around to look at her and my pulse froze.

She was farther back than I expected, on her knees, and leaning against a rocky outcropping as if it were the only thing keeping her from completely collapsing to the ground. Her eyes were closed and even from this distance, I could see her breathing was short and shallow.

Shit. I should have paid closer attention to her.

I knew the spell had affected her. She hadn't been able to stop shaking since we'd left the temple, and her complexion had been pale and hadn't warmed up from the exertion of walking.

I rushed back to her and before I could even reach her, I was hit with the scent of her arousal.

Oh, fuck.

I was instantly hard, my balls aching and my wolf straining to break free. She was mine and she needed me.

My fear for her surged and I shoved it, along with the overwhelming desire to fuck her senseless, as far back as I could.

This couldn't be happening. Not in the middle of nowhere.

"Audrey," I murmured, kneeling in front of her and cupping her cheeks between my palms, urging her to look at me.

Her scent wrapped around me, sweet and heavy, and my wolf heaved, straining to take control. Sweat slicked her too-hot skin, pasting loose strands of hair to her forehead and cheeks, and she shook as if she were freezing. Her eyelids fluttered, cracking partially open, and I could see her pupils were fully blown and she couldn't focus on me. She probably couldn't focus on anything.

All of that were signs of a strong heat fever.

Damn it. I should have refused to try the spell and kept her in Stonehaven, should have insisted she spend her heat with Wilder at the heat clinic. He would have been able to manage her heat and not let it get so bad that she succumbed to the fever.

The urge to claim her, relieve the pressure that I'd been told was tearing her up inside, squeezed my chest. It didn't matter to my wolf that we didn't have shelter or any other comfort — like a bed — his instincts said she was ours and she needed us. Now.

Bishop. Knox. Get back here, I mentally called to them as a snap of power escaped my control and rushed through our connection.

What happened? Bishop asked, his mental voice sharp with worry, knowing if my control on my power was slipping that it was serious.

Her heat. I dropped both packs and gathered her into my arms, heat radiating from her body and her scent suffocatingly strong. *She's got heat fever.*

You said her heat was done, Knox snarled as he bolted toward me with Bishop close behind.

She said it was over, Bishop insisted.

But she's never had a heat before. Realization hit me. If she'd never had a heat before and heats weren't as strong in her realm, then she didn't know that they ebbed and flowed. Sex helped to relieve the pressure, sometimes for a few hours, sometimes for a few days. Of course, her heat had been going since we'd left town ten days ago, so it would have made sense for her to assume no symptoms meant it was over.

Shit, Bishop hissed as if he, too, had figured out what had happened.

I turned and raced south, passing my brothers, knowing they'd grab the packs and catch up.

Heat fever was serious and only the strongest female shifters experienced it if they didn't properly take care of their heat.

I didn't know if this meant Audrey was actually strong and her powers were imprisoned by the curse or if this was a result of our realm changing her body. It could also be the lure of the mating bond or the spell we'd just tried setting it off.

Hell, it could have been none of the above or any combination thereof.

What I did know was that I had to get her safe and

comfortable because a heat fever could last a few days and be rigorous even with two or three partners.

And given that she couldn't have sex with Knox and hadn't given me permission to help, it was going to be up to Bishop to see her through this.

How could you let this happen, Bishop? Knox demanded. *You walked with her all morning. Even if you wanted to get the spell done, you didn't say anything after.*

I didn't know, my brother replied as he and Knox caught up to me with our packs, and I picked up the pace.

"She was shaking," I told them, "but I didn't think it was a fever. I thought it was a reaction to the spell."

"There's no point in laying blame—" Bishoped started but Knox cut him off.

"Yes, there is. If you'd been paying attention, we wouldn't have left Kelna and she wouldn't be faced with suffering in the middle of nowhere."

He shoved Bishop into a boulder, drawing a grunt of pain, and bared his thankfully still-human teeth.

"Control yourself." I released a sharp snap of power, making Knox huff and Audrey whimper. "You can't afford to break the collar. Not while she's got the fever. You could barely control your wolf when she just had regular symptoms."

"Fuck," he hissed.

I glanced at him, trying to determine if he was angry that he had to stay in control or not. "If you want to try Bishop's plan B then you need to keep your cock to yourself."

Audrey moaned, her fingers clenching my shirt, and she buried her nose in my shoulder, instinctually seeking my scent.

Knox roared and rammed his fist into the rock beside him, making Audrey whimper again and curl in on herself.

"We might not be able to get the fever under control at our camp in the abandoned village," Bishop said.

"We need to get to Kelna," I replied. The village that had graciously given us a cabin the other night was the best place for her. We'd have privacy and access to food, water, and shelter. We wouldn't have any of that at the abandoned village where we'd camped last night and there would be limited ways to bring her fever down at the camp as well.

The question was if Audrey would last the day it would take to run to Kelna.

BISHOP

WE RAN THE REST OF THE DAY, ALL THROUGH THE NIGHT, and reached the small one-story cabin on the outskirts of Kelna by midmorning. The village leader had said we could have the cabin again tonight as a rest stop on our way home, and I could only pray he'd let us stay until Audrey's heat was over.

I'd heard about heat fever. It was part of our basic education all pack children had to take, although I'd never seen it firsthand. That was Nova's area of expertise, as well as Wilder's and anyone Wilder employed. But I hadn't thought it would be so bad.

Audrey huddled in Cyrus's embrace, shivering and sweating and whimpering and panting. Her eyes had cracked open periodically during our mad dash back here, but they were always glassy and unfocused, and I wasn't sure if she was even conscious.

Cyrus marched up the wooden steps leading to the

wide porch and the cabin's door, and I hurried ahead of him and opened the door so he wouldn't have to adjust his hold on her.

He'd refused to hand her off, and while she wasn't much heavier than two of our packs combined, she'd soaked her shirt with sweat, along with the front of his shirt, and had blanketed him in her scent. A scent that had me partially hard despite trying to keep my distance and staying downwind. It had been difficult enough for me to concentrate on getting back here as fast as possible and not letting my wolf succumb to her arousal. I couldn't imagine how hard it must have been for Cyrus.

With a nod of thanks, he carried her straight into the bathroom, and I dropped my pack and Audrey's just inside the door then glanced back at Knox.

He'd stayed a good fifty feet away from her the entire run and now stood at the bottom of the steps, glaring at the inside of the small cabin as if he were furious with it... or actually thinking about entering.

His frustration and anger seethed through our twin bond along with a stomach-churning fear, and I was shocked Cyrus's collar on his wolf still held.

Even bolstered with my power, Knox's wolf was a force of nature and one whose mate right now was in trouble. It was a miracle his human half was still lucid.

His hands clenched into fists, but I couldn't tell if that was just his anger or him working up the nerve to follow Cyrus inside.

The cabin wasn't very big, but the main room was

open and had good-sized windows that let in a lot of light. He could probably last a few hours, maybe even a little more before his claustrophobia forced him back outside.

But that would have been on a good day, and today wasn't a good day.

With a snarl, he dropped Cyrus's pack on the deck and retreated deeper into the glade surrounding the cabin.

Bishop, Cyrus called, jerking my attention back to the immediate problem. *We need to bring down her temperature enough for you to explain what's happening.*

I hurried into the bathroom to find her sitting on the floor propped up against the wall. Water poured from the tap into the stone tub that was big enough for her but not for me or my brothers, and Cyrus had already pulled off her soaked shirt.

Her breathing had turned short and shallow and her fingers clenched the front of his shirt. With a soft moan, she strained her neck forward, her lips seeking his.

"Help me get her pants off," he said, his voice gruff and his expression pained.

I hurried to help and undid the tie keeping her pants on as he grabbed her around the waist and lifted. The movement made her whimper, and she leaned into him, her mouth brushing along his collarbone just above his shirt.

A growl rumbled in Cyrus's chest, low, barely audible, and we both pretended it hadn't happened. Quickly, I pulled her pants below her ass and Cyrus set her back down then retreated out of reach before I'd even gotten her pants down her legs to her boots.

"I need to let Rafe know we're back early and that we'll be staying a few days." His gaze swept down her body and the muscles in his jaw flexed. "Let me know what you need."

"She's going to need fluids and something easy to eat. At least until I can get the fever under control," I told him as I unlaced her boots and pulled them off.

Audrey tipped her head back and groaned, her hands sliding to her breasts to play with her nipples.

My half-hard cock stood up to full attention despite my worry for her, and Cyrus grunted and left. The next few days were going to be difficult for all of us and I didn't begrudge Cyrus retreating.

He might not think of Audrey as a potential mate, but I knew he was concerned about her — and not just because she and Knox were bound to each other. He'd been furious to learn she'd hidden her blistered feet from us because that meant he hadn't known she'd been in pain, and he'd been protectively watching her from a distance since he'd learned she had absolutely no survival skills.

I quickly unwrapped the bandage around her calf and checked the three scars and dozens of stitches that marked where the grimalkin had slashed her. The elixir had done its job and she'd been healed in record time. We were going to have to pull the stitches out soon, but after I'd gotten her lucid enough to understand what needed to happen and to relieve some of the pressure of her heat building in her body.

I unwrapped her feet — also healed — and set her in the tub. Audrey cried out when the cool water touched her too-hot flesh and clutched at my arms. Her shivering turned violent, and her breath short and sharp between her chattering teeth.

"It's okay," I cooed, wrapping an arm around her to keep her head out of the water. "It's going to be okay."

I didn't want to tell her that her body was going crazy, and she was going to beg for sex, never being fully satisfied until her heat was over.

She'd been a virgin three days ago and had blushed when she knew we'd been able to scent her arousal. Sure, she hadn't been a naive teenager, but she was still shy and inexperienced.

Her reaction to an uncontrolled heat could go two ways. She'd accept what was going to happen or be mortified by it.

She shivered and moaned, and I brushed her hair back from her face.

"I need you to open your eyes, Audrey." I didn't want to start relieving the pressure without her knowing what was going on.

But her breath picked up and her hips started rocking. A whimper escaped her lips and she fondled her breasts again, searching for a release that would be much easier to get with a partner.

Fuck. I wanted her consent. I didn't want to assume because we'd had sex the other night that this was okay. But there weren't any other options. I needed to break her fever long enough for her to be lucid and to do that, she needed an orgasm.

In truth, unless she wanted to seal her mating bond with Knox, Cyrus and I were her only options to get her through this. And from Cyrus's reaction, it looked like he was going to leave it all to me.

I suppose she could ask for one of the villagers. Maybe it would be better if she went through this with someone she'd never see again.

The thought made my wolf heave inside me. *We* were the ones who were supposed to help her. She was ours. Ours to protect and love. And right now, she needed both protection and love.

I pushed my free hand into the water and teased my fingers over her stomach and into her curls. Her breath hitched and her back arched, pushing her breasts up in invitation.

A low rumble rattled in my chest, my wolf rising to the surface but thankfully not taking control, and with a groan, I dipped forward. I sucked on her closest nipple and slid a finger between her folds, drawing a loud moan that was half pleasure and half relief.

Arousal still slickened her channel despite the water, and I slowly pumped my finger in and out of her. Her hips rocked up to meet me every time I plunged inside her and her fingers tangled in my hair, holding me against her breast.

Her moans grew louder and her rocking sped up, urging me to go faster. I added a second finger, pressed my thumb against her clit, and picked up my pace.

The cool water sloshed in the tub, slapping me in the face, spilling over the edge, and soaking the front of my shirt and pants. I abandoned her breast, earning a whimper of displeasure, even as she bucked faster, but moved to her mouth and was rewarded with a sharp gasp.

I plunged my tongue between her parted lips, matching my pace with my fingers. My cock throbbed, so hard it was painful, but I resisted the urge to pull her from the tub and impale her on it. If she agreed to more, I'd have plenty of opportunities to be inside her, to feel her slick heat clenching around me like it had the other night.

Then her channel started to flutter, indicating she was close, and I ground down on her clit. A second later she cried out her release, her back arching away from the tub and her muscles clenching around my fingers.

I pumped through it, trying to draw it out for as long as possible, as she panted into my mouth. Then she collapsed back against the tub, her body limp, and her eyelids fluttered open.

Thank the Sisters!

"Audrey," I said and her gaze drifted to me, her eyes still a little glassy, her pupils blown wide with desire, but she did manage to focus on me.

"Bishop?" A shiver rushed through her, drawing a moan, and her hips started rocking again, trying to draw out more pleasure from my fingers still buried inside her. "What's wrong with me?"

"You have heat fever," I said, letting her fuck herself on my hand. "It's the worst case scenario for a heat."

"But I thought it was over." Another shiver rolled down her body and her lips parted on a soft moan. "I wasn't going crazy with need after we—" A hint of a blush colored her pale cheeks even as she continued to use my fingers, and she squeezed her eyes shut. "What does this mean?"

"It means to keep the fever from overwhelming you and endangering your life, you need to have sex." I offered her a gentle smile. "Will you let me help you?"

AUDREY

I SQUEEZED MY EYES SHUT, TRYING TO CONCENTRATE ON Bishop's words, but that only made me more aware of his fingers buried inside me and the ache in my core that I couldn't relieve.

A shiver of a climax teased me, and I bucked faster against his hand, chasing it, desperate to make it bloom into a full orgasm.

"Audrey," Bishop said, cupping my cheek and tilting my head up, the precursor to a kiss.

I pried my eyes open, but he hadn't dipped close to kiss me and still watched me with pained concern.

"My fingers and mouth will help, but not as much as direct intercourse."

The promised climax I'd been chasing slipped away as if proving his point, and I whimpered in frustration.

"This could last for a few days and you might be delirious for most of it," he continued.

"But you'll take care of me?" I asked, my voice trembling with cold and need. God, I was losing my mind. I *needed* sex like I needed to breathe.

"I'll always take care of you," he said. "I just want you to understand what's going on." He brushed his lips against mine, finally giving me the kiss I desired.

It was just a whisper of contact, but it stole my breath and shot searing need straight to my core as if it had been more.

The bathroom — how'd we get back to the cabin in Kelna? — darkened and lurched, and I dropped my fingers to my clit, trying to get the heat to break and bring me relief.

"I've got you," Bishop murmured and he curled his fingers inside me, hitting a spot that made my muscles clench and sent light flashing behind my eyelids.

But the relief only lasted a few seconds before the ache returned and I was panting and rocking my hips again.

I tried to figure out what had happened, how I'd been stupid enough to think my heat was over, but I couldn't think past the need consuming me. It burned me up from the inside, overwhelming any attempt to focus.

"Come on," he said, pulling his fingers from me.

I whimpered at the sudden emptiness, my core thrumming, needing, desperate to be filled.

"Just hold on for a minute." He yanked off his shirt, revealing his stunning, sculpted physique then stood and dropped his pants.

His cock sprang free, standing at full attention and making my pulse stall and my mouth dry in anticipation. He was thick and long and bigger than I expected. I couldn't believe I'd had *that* in me the other night. No wonder he hadn't let me see or touch it. I would have gotten even more nervous for my first time and it wouldn't have been nearly as enjoyable.

And now all I could think about was wrapping my fingers around him and licking the glistening drop of precum from his tip.

I reached for him, eager for that taste, but he picked me up before I could grasp him. Water rushed from my body and poured over his hips and thighs, but he didn't seem to care. He carried me out of the bathroom, through the open-style kitchen-living room, and into the bedroom.

The room was furnished like the rest of the cabin with well-used, worn furniture, and the blanket, the linens, and the curtain on the window were mismatched, giving it a homey, lived-in feel. Someone had set out towels for us at the foot of the bed along with a pitcher of water and two glasses on the nightstand.

Shivers wracked my body, but I didn't know if they were from the fever burning me up or the anticipation of having Bishop inside me again.

"I promise I'll always take care of you," Bishop murmured, capturing me with one strong arm behind my waist to steady me on my feet and drying my back with a soft towel.

His hard length dug into my belly and the ache in my core burned hotter.

Moaning, I leaned into him, savoring his scent of fresh-cut grass and comfort, and slid my hands over his wet skin. My fingertips traced over his rippling ads before I dipped them lower, following the V at his hips down to his cock, and wrapped my fingers around him just like I wanted.

A deep, masculine groan escaped his lips, ratcheting up my need, and I teased my fingers up his length and slid them through the precum leaking from his tip.

"Fuck, Audrey," he gasped through clenched teeth. "I can't lose control. I don't want to hurt you."

"I don't care," I begged.

"I know you don't, beautiful. But still—" He palmed my mound and his fingers slid through my folds and slick arousal.

My body bucked into him, eager, needing, desperate, and I tightened my grip on his cock. "I need you. Please, Bishop."

With a groan, he captured my lips in a searing kiss and pushed me back onto the bed. I gasped into his mouth, my breath ragged, and his slickened fingers found my clit. More shuddering need and desperation roared through me, and I clawed at his head and shoulders. More. I needed more. So much more.

"Bish—" My core clenched, relief flooding me as I spun on sensation and light.

But just like the orgasm in the tub, the feeling didn't

last. I couldn't reach the top, couldn't fall into satisfied bliss. I was consumed with a hunger that just couldn't be satiated.

Tears pricked my eyes. I didn't want this.

Please. How do I reach the finish line?

How long was it going to last? And was every heat in this realm going to be like this? I'd go insane.

Bishop pulled his hand away, the sudden absence of his touch making me sob. He hadn't even been inside me, but his retreat felt like a rejection. God, it was so much worse than Knox. Bishop had promised to protect me, take care of me, and now—

His cock pressed into my entrance and my spiraling thoughts lurched.

Oh, yes. Please, yes.

A mini climax shuddered through me, growing stronger with every inch he slowly pushed into me. It crashed into a full-blown release when our pelvises pressed together.

"Fuck," Bishop groaned, his body trembling.

He squeezed his eyes shut and sucked in long breaths, trying to get himself under control. But he was staying perfectly still to do it, and I just couldn't stay still, not long enough for him to get a hold of himself, not even for a second.

I needed more, stronger, faster. I had to move, had to feel his incredible cock sliding along the walls of my channel, building my desire higher and higher.

My hips rocked, moving the fraction they could with him pinning me down.

God, please. I need him to fuck me into oblivion.

I clawed at his powerful shoulders, digging my nails into his flesh, and strained to satisfy myself. But I couldn't get enough movement or friction.

Then Bishop growled low in his throat and opened his eyes. Darkness had flooded his irises, making the green flecks stand out in sharp contrast. His wolf was at the surface of his consciousness, if it hadn't already taken over.

"Fuck me," I begged, not caring if I was talking to the man or the beast. *Just please, fuck me.*

With a snarl, he withdrew and plunged back inside me. Hard. The impact shuddered up my body in a delicious wave that pulled a moan from my throat.

That seemed to be the permission he needed because he grabbed my hips, withdrew, and thrust back in again.

I bucked up to meet him, the impact reminding me of the wild sex with my dream Knox.

In the back of my mind, I was pretty sure my body wasn't ready for even a fraction of the aggressive sex I'd had in my dreams, but I didn't care. Nothing could stop the need screaming through me.

Bishop's fingers dug into my flesh hard enough to leave bruises, but that pain felt so good and there wasn't any other, not like I'd expect for having sex for the second time in my life. Only pleasure.

He pounded into me, spinning me tighter and tighter.

I panted and moaned and begged for more. More more more.

The wave building inside me was stronger than even the ones I'd fantasized about in my dreams, and I clung to it as it took me higher and higher.

It broke with an eruption of bliss that crashed through me. Every muscle in my body clenched tight and stars exploded behind my eyes. It spun me around and around, darkness and light snapped through my vision, shot through every hyper-sensitive nerve, and rang in my soul.

A golden nimbus filled me and I was weightless, floating in bliss, warm and safe. I was home. Exactly where I was supposed to be.

Because Bishop was mine.

CYRUS

AUDREY SCREAMED HER RELEASE, AND I SQUEEZED THE handle of the cold cupboard and gritted my teeth, my cock still painfully hard. I was going to have to take care of myself before I did something stupid like run into the bedroom when she started begging for round two — something my wolf really wanted to do.

A moment later, Bishop groaned his own release, and I'd never in my life been more jealous of my younger brother.

If Knox and I— Hell, who was I kidding? If *I* took care of everything else — since Knox wouldn't talk to the townspeople to get supplies and needed to stay as far away from Audrey as possible — Bishop would be able to focus entirely on Audrey, and she wouldn't need my help to survive a heat that had reached a fevered level.

And really, it was better that I kept my distance.

I didn't have her consent, and even if I did, having sex

with her would muddy the line between us. The line I'd been working hard to make absolutely clear.

She couldn't be my mate and given how she'd been about sex before the fever hit, I knew sex meant something important to her. She wouldn't have sex just to have sex and that meant having sex with her could give her the wrong impression about my intentions.

I heaved my attention back to the cold cupboard, taking stock of the handful of fruits and vegetables, the block of cheese, and the pitcher of dark green juice inside. It wasn't much, barely enough for the evening meal the villagers thought we'd need when we were supposed to return later today.

They were probably going to bring something over around dinner time like they had at breakfast the other day.

I should have looked for Rafe the second I'd left the bathroom like I'd told Bishop I would, but I hadn't been able to get very far before my worry about her condition forced me back. I needed to know she and Bishop were going to be all right first. Then I could look for the magistrate and his wife so I could beg for more of their kindness to let us stay the few days it was going to take for Audrey to get through a heat that shouldn't have been so bad.

Although maybe it had been inevitable.

Audrey wasn't from this realm and she'd already gone into her heat touch-starved —seriously touch-starved for someone from this realm. The fact that she'd said heats in her realm were almost non-events and how her body had already been on the verge of a normal heat before we'd even left Stonehaven should have been a clue that our realm was changing her.

I should have known even though she was an almost powerless shifter that she'd have the mother of all heats. And for all I knew, her incomplete mating bond with Knox could be making it worse.

Bishop stepped out of the bedroom with a set of long dark pink scratches trailing over his biceps. She must have drawn blood for them to be that dark. If she hadn't, his natural healing would have healed the marks before he'd even left the bedroom. He carried one of the towels I'd set on the bed, dropped it in a heap by the bathroom door then sagged onto one of the sturdy wooden chairs at the worn kitchen table.

"She asleep?" I asked, unable to keep my wolf's growl from my voice. I kept my back to Bishop, fighting to get my cock to calm the fuck down, and pulled an apple and a hank of grapes from the cold cupboard.

"And her fever is down a bit," he said. "I also managed to get her lucid enough to explain what was going on."

"Good." I sucked in a slow breath, determined to get myself under control, but that only filled my nose with a mixture of her fresh sweet scent and thick heady arousal.

Fuck it.

I was a guy and Audrey had been giving off pheromones like crazy since her fever hit. It'd be a miracle if I *wasn't* hard right now.

There was no way I was going to get through one day with the cabin smelling like her and sex, let alone three or four days without a hard-on. I was just going to have to accept that and move on — preferably to the bathroom where I could jerk off and relieve the pressure.

I turned to face Bishop and set the fruit on the table. His gaze dipped to the massive tent in my pants, and he cocked an eyebrow but thankfully didn't comment. Then he turned his attention to the food.

"We're going to need more than fruit," he said.

"I was just taking stock before finding Rafe and telling him what's going on," I replied as I filled a glass with water and slid it to him. "I'll go hunting after that. Hopefully, I'll catch something big enough to last the duration since you and Audrey are going to need meat to keep your strength up."

"I left a mess in the bathroom," Bishop said, downing the glass of water and standing. He was at half-mast again, Audrey's pheromones affecting him just as much as they were affecting me.

Except he can do something about it.

You can, too, my wolf told me. *You should. She needs you.*

I shoved that thought aside. Bishop was going to be her mate. I was just going to be her brother-in-law. I shouldn't help her. Not the way I wanted to.

I turned to the cupboards and pulled out a large blue ceramic bowl so Bishop could bring some of the fruit into the bedroom and wouldn't have to make a trip back into the kitchen.

"I'll clean up the bathroom. You go rest. We've been up for over a day and we have no idea how aggressive her fever is going to get." I put the rest of the grapes, two more apples, and a couple handfuls of blueberries in it and handed it to him. They still needed an actual meal with meat, but it was a start. "Next time she wakes, get her to eat something."

Bishop nodded, his expression tight with concern, and returned to the bedroom.

I sucked in another breath filled with the scent of Audrey and sex and went to clean up the bathroom. Depending on how her heat went, she might need more time in the bath or want to clean up in the shower.

Bishop had left his wet clothes and a puddle on the floor and hadn't drained the tub.

The memory of Audrey in my arms, clinging to me and breathing in my scent, her nose nuzzling my neck, her hot body pressed against mine as I carried her shot a burst of white-hot need straight to my cock.

She'd been in distress, her beautiful eyes squeezed tight, and strands of dark blond hair stuck to her sweaty forehead, and my wolf was going crazy, every protective instinct I had howling inside me.

She needed someone to fuck her.

And that someone was Bishop. Only Bishop.

But even though I knew that, I couldn't convince my wolf — or myself for that matter — that helping Audrey through her heat wasn't my job.

She's perfect, my wolf said. *A protector. A mother. Ours. She'll feel so good.*

The thought of pushing into her tight warmth made my balls ache.

We'd make her feel good, give her what she needs. A heat fever this strong is dangerous. We need to protect her. We need to mate with her.

I forced myself to my knees before my wolf could walk us into the bedroom and claim Audrey and shoved my pants down.

My cock sprang free, red and angry, precum leaking from my tip. I squeezed the base, fighting to get myself under control, but the only control I could muster was not going to her.

Fuck me. Why did she have to have the fever? I should have told her and Bishop to fuck every night since she'd started to fall apart on the second day of this stupid journey. All of this could have been avoided.

But she'd been a virgin and shy, and I'd thought if we dealt with her being touch-starved, everything would be fine. She wasn't a strong shifter. Her heat should have never reached a fevered level.

I roughly jerked my hand up and down my length, my grasp so tight it edged on painful.

Now we were stuck here for the next three or four days when we really needed to get back to Stonehaven. The longer we stayed, the greater the chance Knox would succumb to the lure of their mating bond and seal it, destroying any hope of Bishop's slim-to-none plan B.

That, and I couldn't put off my pack responsibilities for much longer. We still had an increase in beast activity in the area along with the strange rip to Audrey's realm in Anakar that could be dangerous.

And while I knew Nova and Deacon could handle most of the day-to-day operations of the pack, I also needed to get home to put some distance between me and Audrey.

My hips jerked forward, fucking into my hand with fast, aggressive thrusts as my wolf thought about how Audrey would pant and moan and then scream her release like she had for Bishop.

My balls tightened and tingles shot up my spine. I came hard, thick ropes of cum spurting into the water on the floor and a strangled cry caught in my throat.

Fuck me. I wasn't sure I was going to be able to wait until we got to Stonehaven to put distance between us.

CYRUS

AFTER I CLEANED THE BATHROOM, I GOT OUT OF THE CABIN as fast as I could, before Audrey's scent could make me uncomfortably hard again, and found Knox pacing a trench in the ground in front of the porch.

His posture was so tight, I was afraid he'd pull something, and when he wrenched around to march my way, I could see his eyes were wild — but thankfully not dark with his wolf.

By some miracle, the collar was holding. The question was, for how long?

"I should have known," he snarled at me. "Everything else about her is fucked up. Of course her heat would be the worst-case scenario."

"Bishop's got it handled." And just Bishop. No matter what my wolf wanted.

"Like he handled her heat before?" He clenched and

unclenched his hands and his lips curled back in a snarl in an obvious challenge.

"We should have known, but we didn't," I told him, my wolf heaving to take control and put Knox in his place for daring to challenge us. He might be *an* alpha, but I was *the* alpha, and I had the strength to prove it.

But that wouldn't help him calm down and I needed him calm to keep the collar intact. Because when it broke, his wolf would take over and not care if Knox wanted to be mated to Audrey or not.

"I'm going to find Rafe and let him know we're here and that we need to stay. Then I'm going hunting. Come with me." Maybe putting some distance between him and Audrey would help.

"I can't hunt as a human." His gaze jerked to the cabin door and the muscles in his jaw flexed. "And I can't leave her."

"You can't fuck her, either," I warned. "She won't be lucid enough to say yes or no, and she has her hope set on Whil being able to transfer the bond."

"I'm not going to ruin any chance she has of getting rid of me." But he didn't look away from the cabin.

How much of his feelings were because of the bond and how much because he actually cared for her? He didn't like being around people, but that didn't mean he didn't have feelings. While he'd kept his distance from her and refused to talk to her, he'd spent the entire trip watching her.

Did he see what I saw? Did he see a shy, uncertain

woman who'd been beaten down her entire life? And did he see how hard she was trying to keep up and be brave and face a realm filled with things she'd never experienced before?

Probably. He wasn't dumb. He just couldn't stand crowds or closed off spaces.

"Just hunt with me. Even if you stay in human form it'll help control your wolf from breaking the collar."

He turned his wild-eyed gaze back to me, his expression stricken. "The bond won't let me leave her. Not when she's like this."

"Are you going to be able to stay away from her?" I didn't want to force him to go with me, but we needed meat. I had to go hunting and I needed to know he wasn't going to cause problems for Bishop.

"Yeah." He huffed a bitter laugh and glance back at the cabin, his expression strained. "Never thought my *condition* would actually be good for something."

He stormed to the far end of the porch, jerked around, and came back, resuming his pacing. It set my nerves on edge, but I knew it was the only thing burning off the angry energy building inside him.

"I won't be gone long."

He grunted his acknowledgment but didn't look at me, and I headed down the path into Kelna.

The town was small, maybe five or six dozen houses, but the buildings were bigger than the average "village" house I'd seen in my travels on diplomatic missions with my parents and were well-maintained.

I found Rafe, his wife, Neera, and their daughter and her new husband, along with most of the villagers in the meadow behind the town. The wedding had been two nights ago, but it looked like the festivities were still going.

Both Rafe, the town magistrate, and his wife assured me we could stay as long as we needed and offered to send someone with food right away. I told her I'd collect everything after I'd gone hunting and take it to the cabin since I was positive Audrey didn't want the townspeople hearing her having sex.

The next five days consisted of hunting and picking up baskets of fruit, vegetables, bread, and baked casseroles, and doing my damnedest to stay out of the cabin and the overwhelming scent of Audrey's arousal.

As it was, I still had to jerk off multiple times in the day just to be able to focus. And I *needed* to focus because Knox was hanging on by a thread, Bishop was fully consumed with Audrey, and Audrey was getting worse. Not better.

A heat fever usually peaked at the end of the second day or the beginning of the third, then the need to mate slowly diminished over the next couple of days from every couple of hours to eventually a few times a day, and then the woman's temperature returned to normal.

But Audrey's temperature remained high — thankfully not dangerously high like it had been when it first started but still high — and the duration between matings was getting shorter and shorter.

It was mid-afternoon on the seventh day when I strode down the narrow path back to the cabin with a bundle of clean sheets and towels.

I was tired, having only managed sporadic sleep since we'd returned to Kelna, and the tension in my body made the headache I started two days ago pound behind my eyes. But I couldn't give in and stop. I had to keep taking care of her, and we'd been at the cabin long enough for Audrey and Bishop to have gone through all the clean bedding and towels in the cabin.

It didn't matter that Bishop said she was barely lucid with the biological drive to mate fully consuming her. She could have a moment of clarity at any time and I wanted her to know we were taking care of her.

It made my wolf furious that all we were doing was cooking and cleaning and keeping our gods damned distance so we didn't do something stupid.

I rounded the rocky outcropping and climbed the half dozen shallow steps carved into the stone ground up to the glade and followed the narrow path through the thigh-high grass and wildflowers to the cabin.

Knox lay on the porch swing, his eyes closed, and his breathing slow and steady.

Thank the Sisters!

He'd finally passed out. He'd been pacing and snarling so much in the last few days, I was afraid that even if he didn't manage to break the collar containing his wolf, I was going to have to chain him up. He'd even begged me to do it just before dawn this morning when Audrey was whining and begging and desperate.

When this mess had started, I'd been jealous of Bishop — and a very small part of me still was — but now I was worried for him. I was pretty sure I dozed at least a little last night but every time I jerked awake, he and Audrey had been going at it. Without a doubt, he was getting even less sleep than I was.

I tiptoed onto the porch and cracked open the cabin door. Audrey's sweet fresh scent — a scent that made my wolf sit up, wag his tail, and yip with joy — wafted over me. Then the heady, rich scent of her arousal followed and my cock jerked to attention.

Fuck. Her scent was killing me. Every instinct I had screamed to satisfy her. By satisfying her, I'd be protecting her. And by protecting her, my wolf and I would prove to her that we were a worthy mate.

Because he *had* to have her. She'd do anything for pups who weren't even her own. We wanted a mate like that, a mate who wanted— no *needed* to protect those too small to protect themselves.

Inside, everything was quiet and I prayed that meant Audrey and Bishop had managed to fall asleep.

But I'd only gotten a few steps inside when the bathroom door opened and Bishop stepped out. He looked tired and worried, and even with the air thick with her sweet scent and heady arousal, he was only at half-mast — which meant he was as exhausted as he looked.

"Tell me you have more of that broth," he whispered.

"Did she drink it all?" Well, that was a miracle.

He hadn't been able to get her to eat anything and she was barely drinking water. And while the heat put her body in a state of conservation, that was only supposed to be for a few days and even a normal shifter with a normal fever came out weak and dehydrated. Which was why the pack tried to avoid letting a heat get to the fever stage and why Wilder and Nova had set up the heat clinic.

"Unless there's a pot in the cold cupboard I can't see, she's had it all." Bishop's expression darkened and he glanced at the partially open bedroom door. "But even if you make another batch, she's not going to be able to last much longer."

"Maybe that means the fever is almost over."

He shot me a hard look. Yeah, I didn't really believe that, either, but I couldn't let Bishop lose hope. He was the one who had to hold it together. Without him, Audrey's heat would never break.

He shuffled to the couch and sagged onto the worn seat cushion. "I have no idea how Wilder does it. I think I've gotten two hours of decent sleep in the last three days, and now it takes half a dozen orgasms to ease the fever long enough to give her ten minutes of peace."

"Wilder doesn't do it alone," I reminded him even as my wolf strained against my control. Bishop wasn't enough. Audrey needed us, too. "And this should have been over at least two days ago."

"I know." He raked his fingers through his hair,

pushing it away from his face. "Whatever we're doing? It's not working."

I'd been thinking the same thing all day but couldn't figure out what we were doing wrong. The only thing I could think of that might possibly influence a heat and made Audrey's different from any other heat I'd heard about was her incomplete mating bond.

"It has to be the bond," I said and Bishop nodded his agreement.

"That's what I'm thinking and why the fever isn't breaking." He swiped his hand through his hair again. "What are we going to do? Knox refuses to accept her."

"He's still adamant that she shouldn't be stuck with him." I dropped the towels and sheets on the couch beside Bishop and headed to the kitchen to pull out what I needed to make another batch of bone broth. Because I *had* to do something.

"You know, sometimes she cries for him when the fever is riding her hard."

I knew. I heard her through the open windows. Knox knew it, too, and he usually retreated to the far side of the glade.

But as much as Audrey begged for Knox, that was the fever talking. She'd walked until her feet bled just to try a slim-chance spell to break their bond.

"I'll talk with the village healer about the sedative this town makes."

"Right," he said. "The moss in the nearby cave that

absorbs the death god's power that they harvest and turn into a sedative. You said it even works on shifters."

Which was a miracle in and of itself. So far none of our doctors or researchers had been able to find a sedative that worked with our physiology. Not even Whil had found anything.

Bishop frowned at me. "Sedating her will help me get some rest, but I don't know if it'll break her fever."

"I'm not betting on that. I want to sedate her so we can take her home. If anyone knows what to do with her, it'll be Nova." As much as Nova had always been like a bratty little sister to me, she was a brilliant physician. Between her and Wilder's experience with hundreds of heats, surely they'd be able to figure out something that didn't involve her sealing her bond with Knox.

"Do you think sedating her will be enough?" he asked as a soft gasp and pained mewling came from the bedroom. His expression tighten, the worry in his eyes deepening, and he shoved up to his feet. "I don't know how many days she has left. She's already so weak."

"Neither of them wants the bond," I insisted even though we all knew the odds of Whil being able to transfer the bond to Bishop were just as slim as the spell that had failed. We had to try. That was what she wanted. "Sealing it has to be our last resort."

"If we can catch her in a moment of lucidity, I can ask her to bond with me," Bishop said. "Maybe that—"

"There's no guarantee she'd have the strength to form a

mating bond and no guarantee that a new bond would break her fever," I said stopping him before he finished, knowing exactly where his train of thought was taking him... because I'd thought the same thing half a dozen times already.

But if a shifter was too close to death, it didn't matter if he or she said the words, the magic for a bond would never spark to life.

The only reason Audrey had been able to bond with Knox, even while she'd been on death's door, was because the mating magic had already been awakened and had been looking for someone to latch on to.

"We'll see how tonight goes and if she doesn't improve, we leave in the morning," I told him. I didn't want to sedate Audrey for seven or eight days, but I would if that was the only way to get her the help she needed.

The mewls turned to whimpering and my chest tightened with worry.

With a groan, Bishop hurried to the bedroom and I caught a glimpse of Audrey writhing on the bed. Her eyes were glassy, staring off into space, her hair was plastered to her forehead and neck, and she panted, short, shallow gasps as if she couldn't catch her breath.

In her consuming need, she'd pushed the sheet down to her hips, and her slight frame looked thinner, frailer. She'd lost some weight with all the physical exertion to walk to the death god's temple and it looked like she'd lost even more. She might not make it to Stonehaven. Not even if we sedated her.

CYRUS

Cyrus!

I woke with a start, my gaze darting over the moonlit glade, searching for what had woken me.

The Sisters were near full, their soft ever-so-slightly pink illumination bathing the long grass and wildflowers and, on the far side of the open space, lay a huddled form whose power felt like Knox's. No one else was around and there was nothing to indicate why I was suddenly awake.

Inside the cabin, Audrey whimpered and moaned, the sound hoarse and strained. She cried out with a strangled sob then almost immediately went back to whimpering, her orgasm giving her no reprieve just like she'd been all afternoon.

I squeezed my eyes shut, trying to will myself to go back to sleep. If we were heading out in the morning, I needed as much rest as possible.

I wasn't sure how I'd managed to fall asleep on the

porch swing the first time with the sounds of the exhausted sex marathon going on or Audrey's scent taunting me every time the wind shifted, but I had, and I needed to figure it out again. It was the only thing I could do.

Fuck. Cyrus! Bishop gasped in my head, his mental voice filled with panic.

I jerked upright, my heart racing. *What's wrong?*

Get the sedative.

Audrey's whimpering grew louder and her moans more pained than pleasured.

Get the sedative now. Please, Cyrus. He groaned and mental whispers of soft, soothing words ghosted through me as he tried to soothe Audrey without breaking our connection. *I can't bring her fever down. I've tried cooling her in the tub. Even put in ice. Nothing is working. She isn't even giving me time to recover.* And I knew without him saying anything that he'd made her come as many times as he could before losing control and coming himself.

I scrambled off the swing as quietly as I could. I didn't want to alert Knox that anything was wrong. His wolf would break his collar and he'd seal the bond without a second thought.

Which would solve our current problem, my wolf snarled at me, pissed that we weren't doing everything in our power to help her.

It's a last resort, I snarled back. If the sedative didn't work then I'd talk to Knox and deal with the consequences — one of which could be Audrey hating me for forcing her to bond with a mate she didn't want.

I hurried inside and grabbed the bottle of sedative and dropper from my pack, grateful I'd visited the town healer right after my conversation with Bishop.

Hurry, he gasped. "It'll be okay. I promise," he cooed, his voice half in my head and half out loud.

Please let him be right, I prayed and raced into the bedroom.

Audrey lay on her side, her arms wrapped around her stomach and her knees pulled up. Desperate, heart-breaking sobs wracked her body and tears streamed over her cheeks onto the pillow.

Bishop lay tucked up against her, stroking her hair and murmuring to her while his other hand was buried between her thighs.

She whimpered and rocked into him, but from the sheen of sweat on her skin and how fast she was panting between her gut-wrenching sobs, I knew the fever was too strong to be satisfied with just his fingers.

Her body tensed and shuddered with a release, but her sobs didn't stop, and Bishop shot me a gutted look, his eyes begging me for help.

Get her on her back, head raised, I commanded and set the bottle of sedative on the dresser, as far away from the bed as possible without leaving the room. I didn't want to risk her fighting me like she had every time we'd tried to feed her.

The sedative had been a gift for saving the villagers

from the grimalkins — just like the use of the cabin — but I suspected it was worth a lot and I didn't want to have to ask for more.

With a steadiness I didn't feel, I unscrewed the bottle, dipped the dropper in the pungent, glowing green liquid, and sucked up the dose for a human female.

When I turned around, Bishop had her partially rolled over, her head in his lap. She was still curled in a ball, hugging herself as if her insides hurt — which they probably did — but at least her head was raised mostly facing up. Hopefully that would mean she'd swallow the sedative and not let it dribble out of her mouth.

I climbed onto the bed, realizing that even in my panic I was fully erect, my cock straining against the confines of my pants... and that Bishop wasn't. Heat radiated from Audrey's frail body like an oven and her eyes stared off into nothing.

"Please," she sobbed. "Please. Why don't you want me? Please. I need—" Her sobs turned to agonized wails and she writhed on Bishop's lap.

I emptied the dropper into her mouth and Bishop followed the sedative with a sip of broth that thankfully encouraged her to swallow.

"Ida said it could take ten to fifteen minutes before it works and only if we've gotten the dose right."

"That long?" Bishop shot me a panicked look.

"Just keep her comfortable," I said, but her breathing turned ragged and her body jerked, her muscles starting to convulse.

Bishop shoved his hand between her thighs again. "We don't have ten minutes."

And Bishop was just too exhausted. Shifters had increased healing and stamina, but even we had limits, especially when we were sleep deprived.

Fuck. The fever had to be brought down long enough for the sedative to work, and I was the one who was going to have to do it.

For a split second, I thought about capturing her attention and getting her consent, but she was too far gone. I wouldn't be able to get her lucid in time to save her... if I could even get her lucid.

Fuck.

Fuck fuck fuck.

I jerked off the bed and yanked off my clothes. My wolf leaped to the front of my consciousness, thrilled we were finally going to do what we should have done days ago, but he didn't take over. He was happy to let me stay in control since he was getting exactly what he wanted.

Bishop watched with a grim expression but didn't say anything. He knew what had to be done, although he didn't know entirely how I felt about it. And he never would.

No good could come from telling my brother I wanted his mate when I shouldn't have her, and without a doubt, Bishop was going to woo her into being his.

I shoved those thoughts aside and tugged on her knees, urging her to open for me.

Her body jerked with another convulsion, and I took

the split-second afterward, when her muscles relaxed, to pry her legs open and shove my hips between them. Bishop had two fingers pumping inside her and they glistened with her multiple releases and her body's need for more.

I watched them slide in and out of her, unable to tear my gaze away. Her breath turned into short, sharp gasps and her hips bucked violently. With a growl, he picked up his pace and ground his thumb on her clit, tearing another orgasm from her exhausted body.

Then he pulled his fingers free and I pushed inside her tight, hot sheath.

Audrey and I both groaned. Audrey with the relief of being properly filled, and me with the relief of finally being buried inside her. I'd been aching for her since before we'd even left Stonehaven, fighting my wolf to stay in control because I couldn't claim her like he wanted.

This was going to be the closest we'd ever get to having her and the circumstances made my soul weep.

A soft orgasm rippled through her, her walls fluttering around my cock, and she weakly rocked her hips, chasing it but unable to make it bloom in full. I slid my thumb over her swollen clit, helping it grow, and was rewarded with a breathy moan and her inner muscles squeezing me tight.

Fuck. I sucked in a breath, fighting the ache in my cock and balls and the need to pound into her and fully claim her. Even if she was mine, she physically wouldn't be able to handle that right now, and I needed to hold out until it looked like the sedative was taking over.

Audrey panted and trembled, her eyes glassy and unfocused. I couldn't stand to see her like that. I wanted her to rise up, embrace the strength within her that I saw every time she squared off against a grimalkin. And I never wanted her to fight one of those beasts again. I was the alpha. It was my job to protect her.

The urge the hold her, comfort her, protect her overwhelmed me, and I pulled her to my chest, my arms around her body supporting her. I hated how light she was, how weak. I hated that she had to walk all the way here, and I hated how the spell failed. Not because I didn't want to share her with Knox or that I thought Knox shouldn't be her mate, but because it had hurt her and had torn a gash in her far-too fragile hope.

I held her still and rolled my hips, sliding in and out in long, slow strokes. She'd already worked herself to exhaustion. I could take over now and do the work, give her what she needed.

Her desperate, sharp pants evened out into deeper breaths that turned into soft moans, and her hands tangled in my hair while she buried her face in the crook of my neck and breathed in my scent.

Another orgasm rolled through her and then another. Her moans grew louder, filled with pleasure, the sound of her satisfaction and her muscles clenching around me, straining my control. A warmth radiated around my heart, our shifter souls connecting and calming. It was as strong as the warmth I felt when my brothers' souls steadied mine... the same strength I'd felt as a child embraced by my mother or fathers.

It was the feeling of home.

And I only felt it because the stress of the situation heightened my emotions, not because it actually meant something.

Audrey came with a weak cry, and I continued to thrust into her, my pace building, my own release threatening to break free.

Another release shook her, strong enough to make her frail body tense against mine, but her cry of pleasure was weaker, softer.

"I think she's about to pass out," Bishop said. He leaned against the headboard, his expression exhausted. He looked like he was about to pass out as well.

His words shattered what little control I had, and I thrust faster and harder, determined to give her one more orgasm before I lost control.

She tried to rock into me, matching my speed, and pulled on my hair. Her lips captured mine in a weak, needy kiss, and my wolf seized control and kissed her back.

He knew I didn't want to cross that line of intimacy and wasn't going to let this opportunity pass him by. Having sex to relieve the fever was one thing, but kissing made it personal, deepened the connection between our souls, and sent searing desire straight to my cock.

She came with a sharp inhalation, her body tensing,

her inner muscles seizing my cock and yanking me over the edge.

I came hard, my seed spilling into her satisfying my wolf even though he knew she was on birth suppressant and this wouldn't give us the pups he wanted.

Then she went limp, the sedative taking over, and I laid her on the bed beside Bishop. He watched me with wolf-darkened eyes, but I didn't see aggression in them from having been with his soon-to-be mate. No, they were filled with understanding.

Yeah. I was so fucked.

KNOX

CYRUS BOUNDED OUT OF THE CABIN IN HIS WOLF FORM AND slipped into the dark forest surrounding the glade.

My pulse lurched. Something had happened. But I had no idea what.

The last time I'd seen him, he'd been sleeping on the porch swing while I'd been trying to sleep on the far side of the glade, as far away from the cabin as the mating bond would let me.

I hurried to the cabin before I realized what I was doing, grabbed the door that Cyrus had left open, and stared inside into the dark living room.

I didn't hear screaming or sex and Bishop wasn't calling me. Audrey had to be okay.

Except she wasn't... and if I didn't want her to be stuck with me with my fucked-up head, I had to let my brothers take care of her.

They had a plan, and I just had to keep my wolf

collared and wait until we were in Stonehaven and Whil had transferred the bond before releasing him.

I shut the door and turned to head back to the far side of the glade but couldn't make myself step off the porch.

The pull of the mating bond mixed with my worries was just too strong. It squeezed my chest, making it hard to breathe and move and hell, just think about anything else.

Fuck, this was my worst nightmare. I hadn't even known that *this* was what I feared the most. But the terror howling and clawing and unable to break free from inside me was stronger than even the squeezing, suffocating panic that seized me if I was inside for too long or surrounded by too many people.

Everything in my soul screamed that I needed to protect her, and my wolf was losing his shit, furious that I'd let Cyrus and Bishop lock him away.

Her heat had been going on for too long and even if I hadn't overheard Cyrus and Bishop's conversation about it not stopping — and the theory that it wasn't going to stop until our mating bond was sealed — I'd be terrified for her.

I curled up on the porch swing, forcing more ice into the mating bond, praying that would help stop me from completely fucking up her life.

I couldn't take care of her the way a mate was supposed to.

I couldn't even cover the basics for a mate.

I couldn't spend more than a few hours inside, and I

couldn't ask her to live like I did, sleeping in the tall grass outside Stonehaven or in the sacred grove outside the alpha's residence. Even if she could shift, she'd still need shelter for winter and the storm season.

But she couldn't shift and she'd want more than just "living inside." She'd want a life and she deserved to have one. She deserved everything her old pack had denied her: friends, family. Hope.

No. I couldn't be her mate. I couldn't be anyone's mate. I was too fucked up.

I squeezed my eyes shut and fought to still my racing thoughts. If the bond wouldn't let me leave the porch, then I needed to embrace the oblivion of sleep. In the morning we'd start the journey back to Stonehaven and then everything would be fine.

Hell, maybe whatever had made Cyrus race out of the cabin as a wolf had been whatever she needed and the fever would be broken by morning... and I wasn't going to think too deeply about what that might have been. A heat fever was dangerous and whatever he'd done would have been to protect Audrey.

I sucked in a slow breath then another and listened to the crickets. I could do this. Audrey could do it. Everything was going to be okay.

A soft thump jerked me awake and I sat up with a start. Inside the cabin, slow footsteps shuffled across the wood floor in an unsteady rhythm, drawing closer. Then a door squeaked and clicked shut, and a moment later, the shower started.

I strained to hear more. It hadn't sounded like Bishop. He was tired, but his steps would have been heavier and surer. Which meant Audrey was in the shower. By herself. Did that mean her heat had broken? Even if it had, she had to be weak. The fever had ridden her hard and she'd barely eaten or slept. Why was he letting her use the shower by herself?

What the hell was wrong with him?

I mentally nudged him and received a sleepy groan in response. Exhaustion and worry surged through our twin bond and I clamped down on it before it could affect me. I hadn't realized just how tired he was.

My wolf wrenched against the collar. If Audrey's fever was that bad, then we needed to go to her, not just to protect her, but to protect the other half of our human soul as well.

I gritted my teeth and squeezed my eyes shut. Bishop wasn't alone. Cyrus might have needed to go for a run, but he'd be back, and Audrey had both of them. They'd be fine.

But my wolf didn't believe that and a growing part of the human me didn't believe it, either.

Something inside *thumped* and all my senses snapped to high alert. Bishop remained asleep and the shower *shushed* in a steady, undisturbed stream of water. Audrey wasn't moving around, that would change the sound of the falling water.

Because she's fallen, my wolf snapped, his voice muted as if he were far away.

A surge of panic shot me to my feet. I wasn't sure if it was mine, my wolf's, or a combination of both. I couldn't assume the thump had been Audrey falling.

And yet given how weak she had to be, I couldn't assume otherwise.

I mentally reached for Bishop to wake him and make him check on her when a soft sob cut through the *shushing* water.

My wolf wrenched me to the door and flung it open before I realized what I was doing.

Panic seized my chest and I gripped the doorframe, stopping my wolf from forcing me inside.

She needs us, he snarled, his voice getting louder, his fear straining the magical collar containing him.

We can't. I tightened my hold on the door, fighting to stay where I was. The wood groaned, threatening to crack beneath my grip, and the walls of the cabin crowded closer together, proving exactly why we couldn't be her mate.

Another sob cut through the sound of the falling water and my wolf wrenched my unwilling body to the bathroom despite the pressure of the collar.

Audrey sat huddled in the corner of the shower just outside of the spray, hugging her knees to her chest. Her hair was wet and limp around her face and shoulders, her body too pale and too thin, and her eyes were squeezed tight in desperate agony.

The pressure in my chest that had been squeezing me since her fever had started crushed tighter, and I sucked in a sharp breath filled with her sweet scent and the scent of her arousal.

All fear of being closed in and suffocated by the small room vanished and my focus narrowed to just her, everything within me screaming to help her.

I turned off the water, crouched before her, and cupped her cheeks in my palms, urging her to look at me.

Her lids fluttered open and she locked gazes with me. Her eyes were surprisingly clear, the fever having eased enough for her to be lucid.

"Knox?" she gasped as tears rolled down her cheeks, the agony in her expression breaking my heart.

It should never have come to this. Bishop should have been taking care of her from the moment we'd left Stonehaven. Except if Bishop and Cyrus's theory was correct, that wouldn't have made a difference.

Only sealing the bond would have prevented this.

Her body tensed and her face scrunched in agony. A strangled moan escaped her clenched jaw and her breathing grew shorter and sharper.

My pulse lurched and I picked her up, not caring that she was getting my clothes wet. Sisters, she was lighter than when I'd carried her on my back to escape Darkweald. And that had already been too light for my liking. It spoke of neglect and too many days going to bed hungry. And now she was wasting away to nothing.

I had to get her to Bishop.

No. I had to end this.

Fuck.

I didn't want to seal the bond, didn't want to trap either of us. But there wasn't any other choice.

I set her on the counter and brushed her damp hair from her face. She stared up at me with her soulful brown eyes, the gold rings around her pupils shining bright, mesmerizing me and reminding me that I'd never been close enough to look her properly in the eyes to notice that subtle, beautiful detail.

The bond had already ensnared my soul, it was only a matter of time before this brave, determined woman fully ensnared my heart.

Before I realized what I was doing, I palmed the back of her head to keep her steady and captured her lips with mine.

Her breath hitched then turned into heavy pants, and she kissed me like she was starving. Her fingers clung to my shirt and her hips rocked up, pressing her slick heat against my painfully hard cock.

My wolf howled and heaved inside me, straining against the collar, determined to break free and claim her. She was ours and we'd neglected our responsibility to protect her for too long. We shouldn't have even left Stonehaven. We should have accepted the truth from the very beginning. She was our mate. She'd always been our mate and we'd just been waiting for fate to bring us together.

I bit back a growl, undid the tie keeping my pants up, and shoved them down my legs. My cock sprang free, jutting between us, and Audrey wrapped her small hand around it.

More tears rolled down her cheeks and she sobbed into my mouth.

"It's the only way," I said, my voice gruff and my throat tight with guilt.

"But you don't want me," she said even as she weakly stroked me and pressed me against her slick, swollen folds.

"I don't want anyone." I captured her lips again, my need for her tearing through the last of my resistance.

I needed her as much as she needed me, needed to fill her and complete myself, needed the bond that would only make us miserable.

I pushed into her, unable to hold back any longer. She moaned, the sound loud and satisfied, just like the sounds she'd made for my brother.

See, I could please her just as well as they did.

I would please her better because she was mine.

I tangled my fingers in her wet hair and tugged her head back, deepening our kiss, as I plunged into her again and again.

"Please, Knox," she begged against my lips. "Harder. Please, please, please."

I picked up my pace, pounding into her as she wept and begged for more, for me.

"Yes," she cried. "I need you, Knox. I need you."

"You're mine," I growled, my wolf straining to break the collar.

A shudder swept through her and her walls clamped around me as her eyes rolled back in pleasure, but I kept pounding into her. I wanted her to scream, wanted to brand my soul onto hers and shatter the fever consuming her. If we were going to make this sacrifice, I was going to save her.

Another orgasm tore through her and her moans grew louder. But the fever wasn't letting go. I could feel it rising again, feel the heat radiating from her skin.

My balls and cock ached, the need to fill her with my seed tightening every muscle in my body. But I needed to hold out, needed to make her come again and again. I needed her screaming my name.

"Who's your mate?" I snarled.

"You," she gasped, another weak climax rippling through her.

She was losing strength, which meant I was losing her.

"Who?" I yanked her hair, determined to get her attention and keep her from succumbing to the fever. Her eyes flew open and her gaze, filled with a wild heat, locked on mine.

"Say my name," I demanded as I pounded into her, my hand behind her butt jerking her toward me with each thrust. "Say. My. Name. Who's your mate?"

"You," she cried, her body trembling, her expression wild with pleasure. "You, Knox."

Every muscle in her body contracted, the force wrenching my own release from me. Heat shot down my spine into my balls, my canines grew despite my wolf being collared, and I sunk my teeth into Audrey's shoulder, claiming her.

She screamed my name again, her voice reverberating into my soul, ringing with a great, powerful gong. Every cell within me vibrated at the sound, aligned, and a brilliant golden light exploded behind my lids.

Mine.

She was mine. Forever.

Gods help me.

KNOX

AUDREY SAGGED AGAINST ME, HER BODY GOING COMPLETELY limp and her breathing turning deep and steady with unconsciousness. The heat from her skin cooled, faster than I would have expected, but then her fever hadn't been a hundred percent natural. It had been spurred on by the magic of our mating bond.

Our now complete mating bond.

Warmth, unlike anything I'd ever experienced before, swelled around my heart, and a sense of calm, of being home, stronger than what I felt when my twin was steadying my soul, surged into the very essence of my being.

How could I have been so stupid to think sealing the bond with Audrey was a bad thing?

It was the most right thing I'd ever done in my life. Even my wolf, while still pissed that he was collared and yearning to claim Audrey again with him in control of our body, was satisfied.

But that still didn't address any of the reasons I couldn't be her mate. How could we possibly have a life together when I lived most of my time as a wolf and she couldn't even shift? I couldn't even spend more than a few hours inside.

That thought made me suddenly aware of the walls surrounding me. The bathroom wasn't the smallest I'd seen, but it was still an enclosed space with one too-small window.

Holding Audrey steady on her perch on the counter, I kicked off my boots, stepped out of my wet pants, and yanked off my soaked shirt. Then I carried her out to the porch, snagging the blanket on the back of the couch in the living room as I walked by.

I should have taken her back to the bedroom and left her with Bishop, but I wasn't ready to let her go. Just holding her was steadying my soul and I needed to stay calm. I had too many thoughts whirling in my head and no answers.

A low growl rumbled in my chest as I wrapped the blanket around us and settled on the porch swing with Audrey cradled in my arms.

She sighed in her sleep and nuzzled her nose into the crook of my neck, taking in deep, slow breaths of my scent while her sweet scent and musky arousal clung to me, fueling the sense of rightness.

Mine. All mine.

Except she wasn't just mine. She and Bishop had feelings for each other, and as much as I wanted to hold her and never let her go, I knew Bishop would be good for her. Better than me.

In fact, I should push him to claim her as soon as possible. Maybe his claim would distract her from our bond and she wouldn't be compelled to be with me.

She could have a normal life.

With my brother.

My wolf heaved against the collar, snarling and snapping his mental teeth at me. Giving her to Bishop and then trying to step away from her life was unacceptable. She was ours. We'd never leave her.

Even if it's best for her?

We're what's best for her, he growled, the collar making him sound far away and muffled.

But we weren't best. Hell, I didn't even know what to say to her when she woke. Even if she hadn't actually been fully lucid and the heat fever prevented her from remembering having sex in the bathroom, she'd know right away the mating bond was sealed. There was no mistaking the sense of completeness, of rightness... of permanence.

It felt so different from the heavy aching cage around my heart and the chain binding us together that had first formed and I'd filled with ice to keep us apart.

Ice and distance that I'd known had hurt her.

And now I really had no idea what to say to her.

Sorry wasn't enough. And neither was an explanation. Now that we were bonded, my reasons felt stupid and yet still so significant.

Fuck. I had no idea what to do. I'd never been in a relationship before. I'd had a few flings, most of them with Bishop at my side, before my wolf had taken over and I'd gone feral. They'd been pity or curiosity fucks, girls wanting to say they'd had the wild brother, the dangerous one. But none of them had been serious.

Hell, none of them had even been casual. How could they have been? I wasn't normal. I was fucked up. I didn't want to meet friends or family. I didn't want to be social and go to parties or dinners or events. I wanted to be left the fuck alone.

Until now.

But alone was the best option for Audrey.

She had a life to build, a fresh start waiting for her in Stonehaven, and my fucked-up head would only stand in her way.

Panic flooded my twin bond and I gritted my teeth, determined to not let it affect me. Bishop was awake and had just realized Audrey wasn't in bed.

I've got her, I told him. *We're on the porch swing.*

The panic shattered, followed by confusion then a stomach-churning mix of emotions flashing so fast they were nearly impossible to recognize as he realized I'd sealed the mating bond.

Yeah. That was how I felt about the whole situation as well.

Why? he asked, his footsteps hurrying across the living room floor and drawing closer to the door.

You know why. Her fever wasn't going to break unless the bond was sealed and now her fever has broken.

The door creaked open and Bishop stood in the doorway looking exhausted. His gaze slid over Audrey curled against me, her expression relaxed and peaceful, and he released a heavy breath.

Thank the Sisters, he said, sagging against the doorframe as the energy from his fear evaporated.

As soon as she's strong enough, you need to mate with her, I told him, even as a part of me roared at the words. She was mine. I was supposed to be able to protect her and fulfill her needs. But I couldn't and I never would.

You still need to develop a relationship with her, Bishop said as if he already knew that I planned to keep my distance after he bonded with her — probably because that's what I did with all the things I couldn't handle. It was always easier to say, 'to hell with it,' and move on. And it would be better for Audrey if I did.

Cyrus, still in his massive black wolf form, bounded out of the underbrush on the far side of the glade and raced toward us, stopping at the foot of the porch steps. His tongue lolled from his mouth and his sides heaved with heavy breaths as if he'd spent the entire time away from the cabin running.

Knox sealed the bond and broke her heat, Bishop said.

Good, Cyrus stepped forward, his form turning liquid for the blink of an eye before solidifying into his human form, and he marched up the steps to the door. *We still leave in the morning.*

Shouldn't we give her a day to recover? Bishop asked.

Cyrus glared at him and Bishop moved to the side to let him pass.

She can recover on the way. The fever might have done more than exhaust and starve her, and we can't chance Kelna's human healer not recognizing if there's a problem.

And while the healing elixir Whil made healed a lot of things, it didn't help with exhaustion, starvation, or rifts between our human and wolf souls. Given how Audrey's connection to her wolf was so buried she couldn't even shift, it wouldn't surprise me if the heat fever had created more problems.

The thought made me tighten my grip on her.

If I hadn't been stubborn, none of this would have happened, and the only way I could think of to make it up to her was to convince Bishop to mate with her as soon as possible and stay the hell out of her life. Our bond was sealed and the overwhelming compulsion to be together was gone.

Audrey bonding with Bishop would overpower any other desires to be with me. It had to.

AUDREY

THE RICH SCENT OF WOOD SMOKE WRAPPED AROUND ME like a comforting blanket and a reassuring calm heat filled my chest. I was safe. I was loved. I was home. The achy, icy hollowness from Knox rejecting our bond was gone and it was never coming back because we'd sealed our mating bond.

Oh, God!

My pulse lurched, grief and horror consuming all my warm feelings.

Knox and I had sealed our bond.

I was now permanently bonded to a man who didn't want me and was furious at me for accidentally bonding with him in the first place.

Tears welled in my eyes and I buried my face into the shirt of whoever held me.

It had all been for nothing. I'd walked until my feet bled and then walked some more, and it had been pointless.

Why couldn't we have held out longer? We'd just needed to get back to Stonehaven and Whil could have transferred the bond to Bishop.

But that had been a long shot. Just like the spell in the death god's temple.

Cyrus had warned me that I was going to have to face the fact that Knox and I were going to be mates, and I hadn't wanted to believe him. We'd been walking away from the temple and I—

My thoughts stuttered. I'd been exhausted and too cold. I—

Images of being with Bishop, of begging him to satisfy me as an agonizing, desperate need clawed at my insides flooded through me. I'd pleaded with him to fuck me again and again. I'd needed more more more, and he'd been all over me and in me, hands, mouth, cock. I could still feel the glorious pressure of him pushing inside me, of how he hit an amazing spot when he pushed in from behind. I'd needed him more than anything and had been relentless in seeking my pleasure.

More tears leaked from my eyes and I clung tighter to the shirt, pressing my face against a hard, sculpted chest.

I'd been an animal, consumed by my need, not caring about anything but having him fill me.

Heat burned my cheeks. I'd lost complete control.

Then Cyrus's face flashed through me and my body burned with the memory of him thrusting into me.

I'd had sex with Cyrus? That didn't make any sense.

Cyrus didn't like me and he certainly didn't want to have sex with me.

Another set of strong hands wrapped around me, and I was pulled into someone else's embrace and enveloped in the scent of fresh-cut grass.

I tried to open my eyes, tried to drag myself to full consciousness and see what was going on, but I couldn't. Exhaustion pulled at me but wouldn't drag me back under and release me from the horror of my memories, and my sobs grew stronger.

A soothing hand stroked my head and a low voice murmured words my whirling mind couldn't register.

All I could think about was how I'd been out of control, how I'd demanded sex again and again from a man I'd wanted to be my mate, how my fantasy of having sex with Cyrus felt so real, and how I was now trapped in a bond with Knox.

Trapped. Forever.

My life in this new realm was over before it had begun, and the thought of being imprisoned in a loveless mating came out in desperate, strangled sobs.

I didn't know what to do.

There was nothing I *could* do.

Finally, my exhaustion dragged me back into darkness, and I drifted into a churning, black sea, bobbing up to catch blurry glimpses of rugged, rocky scenery passing by, small crackling fires, and soothing hands urging me to eat and drink a cloying bitter liquid.

I had no idea how long the darkness held me captive,

all I knew was that every time I broke through, I remember how I'd been, how I'd begged Bishop and Cyrus and Knox to use me in every way possible... or had that been a dream? A nightmare?

What was even true anymore?

Maybe I was dead.

Maybe that monster had eaten me and this was hell. It was just as likely as me actually escaping Sterling and Royce and the pack, falling through a rip between realms, and landing in a place where they couldn't reach me. Even if I had my full shifter powers— Hell, even if I was strong enough to be an alpha, I'd never have the ability to open a rip or gate or anything else between realms.

A dark, menacing laugh rumbled, striking sudden, icy fear within me, and I froze, afraid to move, afraid to look like the prey that I was.

"You're desperate," a voice hissed in my ear, but when I wrenched around to face whoever it was, I found myself alone in my old pack's sacred grove. "Whore."

"It was my heat," I insisted. But that didn't release the shame that sat heavy and hot within me.

"Greedy cunt," the voice hissed in my other ear. "Greedy, desperate cunt. You begged for it. You'll always beg for it. You're begging for it now."

"No." I hugged myself. I wasn't like that. And yet mixed with the shame was desire to be with Bishop again like our first time before my fever, or to be with Knox just like how I'd dreamed, or to have Cyrus hold me with such tenderness as he thrust inside me.

"You're going to beg your mate and he's going to fuck you and still hate you because you're weak."

The words sliced into my soul, bleeding in more shame, while my voice, crying for Knox to give me more, begging him to fuck me, echoed around the grove.

"That," the evil voice said with a dark chuckle, "was a pity fuck. He had to seal the bond to save his life. Not because he loves you."

"The bond will help," I insisted. The bond was supposed to deepen the love between two people, but if there wasn't any love to begin with...?

"You're going to be his convenient cunt. You'll never say no to him and he's going to fuck all his hate into you."

"He won't." He wouldn't. "Bishop would never let—"

The menacing laugh roared around me. "Bishop is his brother. He's family, not some weak pathetic whore. He wants to fuck you with his brother because they're sick fucks and you're the sickest of them all. Do you honestly think two guys would want to share you?"

Was it all a trick? Was Bishop trying to manipulate me just like Royce had when he tricked me into thinking we were fated mates?

My throat tightened and tears burned my eyes. It couldn't be a trick. I believed Bishop. He cared for me. I know he cared for me.

"You're a convenient cunt who won't talk back. You'll take whatever they give you, you'll beg for it, and they'll laugh at how they've turned you into their toy."

"That's not true." Sure, Bishop had talked about sharing me with Knox, but it was to help me... wasn't it?

"You don't want to be used like that," the voice taunted, back to whispering right behind me. "Do you?"

I wrenched around, still alone in the grove where Sterling had tried to sacrifice me.

"You're only good to be a fuck toy or a sacrifice," he mocked.

"No."

"You know it's true," he said. "You can feel it in your soul... along with the bond keeping you prisoner."

"It's not true." Except I was so weak. No one had ever wanted me. Not even my own father. Everything Sterling had told me over all those years had chipped away at me, breaking me down into something fragile that would inevitably shatter.

"You know you only have one option."

I had no options. I was trapped in the mating bond.

"You know what it is." The voice deepened, his tone cajoling. "It's in your DNA."

The image of my father's blood splattered over the yellow bathroom tiles flashed through me.

"No."

"Yes. Unless..." the voice turned wicked. "Unless you do want to be a begging cunt."

"No," I insisted, but I didn't know if it was to killing myself or being Knox's whore. I had more self-respect than that... didn't I?

"You do," the voice whispered. "He hurt you. He hates

you. He fucked you without you saying yes. He and his brother are going to continue to use you. Do it."

"No," I whimpered. I didn't want to give up like that, didn't want to accept that happily ever after was a ridiculous fantasy for someone like me.

"Do. It," the voice screamed.

Something deep within me jolted and I screamed back, "No!" The wildness I'd felt when I'd dreamed of Knox surged. "Hell no."

I wasn't like my father. I was stronger than him, not as a shifter but where it mattered, where it *had* to matter. I might be afraid and ashamed, and I might make myself smaller to avoid being noticed by the predators around me, but I didn't give up.

I never gave up.

I always found another way, even if that meant being patient and suffering while I waited for the right moment.

"No!" I threw my head back and released a half scream half howl.

The wildness rushed through me, spinning me around and around, and the churning black sea pulled me into darkness again.

BISHOP

I GENTLY ROCKED AUDREY IN MY ARMS AS SHE SOBBED uncontrollably, praying her latest dose of sedative would take effect soon.

I had no idea what was going on in her head, but I feared it didn't bode well for how she'd feel when she was fully conscious. I'd been afraid that because she was so shy about sex, she'd be horrified at what her heat had made her do, and it was looking like I was right.

We were going to have to tread carefully with her once Cyrus had decided she'd recovered enough from her exhaustion to stop sedating her and reassure her that there was nothing she should be ashamed of.

If I was smart, I'd arrange for her and Nova to talk when we got back. Audrey might not believe what a bunch of men said about her heat, but she might believe another woman.

It was such a weird thing to be upset about. Naked-

ness and sex weren't something members of our pack
were ashamed or afraid of. But I knew from having met
other races as part of my education in becoming one of
the pack's alphas that that wasn't the case with everyone.
And while Audrey was a shifter, her pack was vastly
different from ours and we couldn't treat her like one. Not
for this.

"We need to pick up our pace," Cyrus said, glaring at
the southern horizon before turning his glare on me.

My wolf bristled, taking his expression as a challenge
and I nuzzled the top of Audrey's head with my cheek, a
subtle reminder to the beast half of my soul that we had
more important things to worry about and that Cyrus
wasn't challenging us. He'd been glaring at everyone and
everything since having sex with Audrey.

Her sobs turned to drowsy tears, her body still trembling against me with her distress and my chest squeezed
so tight it was hard to breathe. I wanted so desperately for
her to be okay, to not worry about anything, but I
suspected she was afraid of what we now thought of her.

She was probably also afraid of her permanent relationship with Knox. Even unconscious, her soul would be
able to sense that the mating bond had been sealed, and
that was another huge thing for her to be afraid of.

"For fuck's sake," Cyrus snapped as he ran his hands
down his face. "Just hold her, Knox. The sedative is about
to take over and she'll be out for at least five hours. She
needs her fucking mate to steady her soul."

Knox tensed. His gaze, like it had been for the last two

days, was locked on Audrey, and a wave of longing washed through our twin bond along with a stomach-churning mix of emotions: need, anger, shame, horror, hope.

He'd been a mess since we'd left Kelna, clinging to her for almost all of the first day, his emotions flipflop-ping between panic and satisfaction when she snuggled close and terror when he realized he was preening at her unconscious attention.

He'd refused to let me or Cyrus carry her until we let the sedative partially release her in order to coax some food into her and she'd started coming to and had begun to cry.

Then he'd really panicked and shoved her into my arms and refused to take her back.

"I don't know what to say to her," he said, rushing down a steep incline as if I were going to throw her into his arms that instant.

"She's unconscious." Cyrus hopped down after him while I took it slowly, mindful of my precious cargo. "No witty banter is required. Hell, no banter at all. Right now, she's perfect for you."

Knox released a sharp growl and leaped at Cyrus, slamming him against a boulder and ramming his fist into Cyrus's stomach.

"Take that back," Knox snarled, his eyes flashing dark for a second as his wolf strained to break the collar imprisoning him.

"Take on your responsibilities," Cyrus spat, shoving

Knox off him with a powerful push that sent my twin
stumbling backward.

"I am." Knox tensed, readying to leap at Cyrus again,
and I shoved my way between them knowing Audrey's
unconscious presence would automatically stop the fight.

"She needs her bonded mate steadying her soul." I
glared at Knox. "She needs to know she'll be loved and
accepted for what's happened even if she's unconscious."

Knox huffed but didn't retreat or resist when I pressed
her against his chest and she snuggled up against him.

The motion made my throat tighten and my wolf rise
to the surface in a strange mix of relief that she'd
accepted him — even if she wasn't fully aware of him —
and jealousy. It didn't matter that I logically knew having
Knox hold her would be best for her. I didn't want to give
up comforting her.

"And you!" I wrenched my glare to Cyrus once I'd
made sure Knox had a solid grip on Audrey and had
forced myself to step away from them.

"Me what?" Cyrus demanded back as he squared his
shoulders in a not-so-subtle reminder that he was bigger
than me.

A ripple of his power escaped his control and I raised
an eyebrow, knowing I didn't need to point out that he
was being an asshole. Something I sure as hell wanted
the reason for but wasn't stupid enough to ask about at
the moment.

I'd ask him later when his wolf wasn't riding him so
hard.

I knew he cared about Audrey, but I would have thought his mood would have improved now that her fever was gone.

He wrenched his power back and pushed past me. "I want to get to the edge of the next forest by nightfall."

The forest that was still so far away we only knew it was there because of the map and the fact that we'd passed through it on our way north. We were going to have to really push our pace if we were going to make it there before the sun set.

But that meant we'd be that much closer to Stonehaven and help for Audrey, help I prayed she wouldn't need.

Maybe when she finally regained full consciousness, she'd have already cried out all of her negative emotions.

Except I knew it didn't work that way. Even if she acted fine and said she was fine, she might not be. I needed to keep an eye on her since Knox had no experience with women and wouldn't have a clue if something was wrong, and Cyrus was hopeless with them and would probably say something to make it worse.

AUDREY

THE NEXT TIME I SURFACED, BISHOP WAS SETTING ME ON A folded blanket on the ground, a large boulder at my back to help me sit upright.

"There she is," he said, his eyes lighting with warmth. "How do you feel?"

He brushed a lock of hair from my face, and I dragged my wavering gaze from him to the fire behind him, my thoughts moving in slow motion. The flames danced merrily, crackling and snapping as Cyrus slowly turned some kind of animal on the spit above it.

Behind him, I could make out hints of rocky land-scape, a thick shrub covered in leaves and small white flowers, and a dark sky with only a hint of light at the very edge of the horizon, indicating that the sun had just set.

"Where are we?" We weren't in the death god's lands — the ground hadn't been this uneven and the shrubs shouldn't have had leaves let alone flowers. That, and I felt like we'd already returned to Kelna, that we should have still been there.

But my thoughts were too fuzzy, swirling around and around, too soft to properly catch, and I couldn't get past when we would have gotten back to Kelna in the first place. The spell at the death god's temple had failed... I'd been too cold... I—

Realization stole my breath and I pressed my hands over my heart. The bond.

"Your heat turned into a fever," Bishop said, his brown eyes searching mine looking for... I didn't know what. Recognition? Remembrance?

There was something there, but it felt so far away, pushed down beneath a viscous sea of darkness.

"The only way to break the fever was to seal the mating bond," he added.

Yes. I nodded slowly, my cheeks burning as some of the memories filtered back in and my stomach twisting with the thought of that horrible dream.

"But don't worry." He sat beside me and pulled me into his lap. The warmth of our shifter connection swelled within my chest, soothing and steadying me. "As soon as you're strong enough, we can bond."

And then I'd be in a second mating bond with a guy I barely knew.

My throat tightened at that. I didn't know why. I felt safe with Bishop, was attracted to him, and knew he'd love me. But that didn't negate the whirling mess of emotions inside me for Knox or the nagging doubt from my nightmare.

My soul said Knox was my mate and always would be. I couldn't just bond with Bishop and forget about him... even if that was what Knox wanted.

The shrub rustled and Knox stepped out from behind it, carrying an armful of branches for the fire.

My gaze instantly jumped to his and I was drowning in the brown depths of his eyes. Even in the darkness with him standing at the edge of the fire's light, I was pulled into those depths.

The heat in my chest billowed stronger as if he were holding me like Bishop was, and the realization that he could affect me like that without touching me stole my breath.

I ached for him. But it wasn't the desperate consuming need that I'd fought before. This was a sadness, a recognition that he wasn't rushing to my side, and a knowing that he still wanted to put distance between us.

But if I looked deep — or perhaps that was if I *sensed* deeper into our bond — I could also see uncertainty.

Of course, he had lots of reasons to be uncertain about me. He was probably still angry that I'd forced the bond on him and that to save me — and hence save himself — he'd had to complete it.

Cyrus huffed, breaking the spell between me and Knox, and handed a canteen to Bishop.

"Drink," he said, shooting me a stern look along with

a ripple of power that thankfully wasn't strong enough to compel me.

I raised my hands to take it from Bishop and realized they were trembling and weak. In fact, all of me was weak and worn out. Was that from the fever? How—? "How long did it last?"

"Your heat fever?" Bishop asked as he helped me drink. "Nine days."

"Nine days?" I gasped. "I've been out of it for nine days?"

"Longer," Cyrus replied without looking away from the fire while Knox took up position opposite me and broke apart the branches into fire-appropriate pieces. "Do you remember? You passed out before we'd even gotten out of the death god's lands. Then it was seven days in Kelna and three more after we left."

"Those last three were aided by a sedative," Bishop said. "The fever exhausted you and you needed to recover."

I motioned for Bishop to help me take another long sip of water, unsure what to say to that.

"So, we're a week away from Stonehaven?" I asked instead.

"Closer to half a week," Cyrus replied. "About five days. We've been pushing our pace."

I guess I really had been slowing them down. And given how weak and shaky I felt, I doubt they were going to let me walk anytime soon.

Not that I was going to be insisting they let me. I'd already embarrassed myself enough during the fever.

The memory of begging Bishop for sex flashed through me and my cheeks heated.

"Hey," he said softly. "None of that." He hooked his finger under my chin and drew my gaze up to his. "Fevers are the worst case scenario for heats. Don't be ashamed of whatever you remember. You couldn't control it and none of us judge you for it."

I glanced at Cyrus, who was now watching me, his expression hard.

"Even if you and Bishop had been mated, Nova still would have sent you to the heat clinic," he said. "It's a miracle he got you through as much as he did."

"And sealing the bond was the only way?" I turned my attention to Knox, but he'd slipped back into the darkness beyond the campfire.

It looked like nothing had changed between us. He was still avoiding me, and while his rejection didn't threaten my sanity, it still hurt, and I still had a feeling we'd come crashing back together if we didn't work something out.

Despite being exhausted, I stayed awake long enough to eat a full serving of dinner — which consisted mostly of meat and fresh greens that the guys had picked up while walking.

Then I drifted off, wrapped in a blanket and Bishop's arms, and was tossed through a lurching montage of having sex with Bishop — sex that wasn't like our soft sweet joining that had been perfect for my first time.

The dreams ended with Knox capturing my mouth and body and sealing our bond with a golden blaze, a resounding gong, and a soul-shattering orgasm.

AUDREY

WITH A GASP, I JERKED AWAKE. A SOFT, WARM THROBBING radiated from my core and for a sudden, fearful heartbeat, I was afraid my heat wasn't over.

But the throbbing was a whisper of what my heat had been before, even when I'd first thought my heat was over. The throbbing now was more like my body remembering what had happened, the sensation spurred on by my dreams.

I didn't know if I should be grateful that those were my only dreams and I hadn't had a repeat of the nightmare or not.

Before me, the fire had burned down to embers and a pot now hung on the spit. Cyrus sat on the other side from me, packing his blanket and three of our four eating bowls into his pack, while Bishop crouched by the fire, stirring our breakfast.

Hints of pink still edged the horizon, indicating dawn

hadn't been that long ago, but I was still a little surprised we hadn't broken camp and headed out already.

Whatever the reason, I was grateful I wasn't going to have to eat breakfast in the early dawn gray, although given that Cyrus was just about ready to go, I was still going to have to rush.

Groaning, I sat up, my muscles still weak and achy from whatever it was that I'd gone through.

"I was hoping you'd wake for breakfast," Bishop said with a heart-melting smile.

He scooped oatmeal from the pot into the last of our eating bowls and handed it to me along with a spoon.

"Thanks," I replied, taking it just as my stomach let out a loud, long growl.

Cyrus sighed at the noise, but it didn't sound like a huff of frustration, more like one of relief, which was very un-Cyrus like.

As I ate — oatmeal with last night's leftover meat and spinach — Knox returned to camp with our canteens, the outsides wet from having just been refilled.

Once again our gazes locked, the moment stealing my breath, and I was falling into eyes so much like Bishop's and yet so very different. Where Bishop's brown depths were warm and inviting, Knox's were filled with something deeper and darker. Longing? Confusion? Frustration?

He opened his mouth and his eyes narrowed. I could tell he wanted to say something and prayed it wouldn't be more rejection. We needed to figure out what was next because whatever it was, we had to do it together.

And as much as that broke a piece of my heart and made me want to scream, it was our inescapable reality.

I didn't want to be mated to someone who didn't want me and would forever hate me for trapping him, but there wasn't anything that could be done about it. We just needed to suck it up and move forward.

And I wasn't going to acknowledge my deepest fear that my nightmare was correct and they were just using me.

The strange look in Knox's eyes deepened and he jerked his attention to Cyrus. "Are you done with the pot?" he asked, setting the canteens beside Cyrus's pack.

"Yes." Cyrus dumped one of the canteens on the fire then handed it back to Knox who took it and the pot and disappeared around a large, rocky outcropping.

"He should have waited until you were done," Bishop said with a sigh and he unwrapped the blanket from around me and shoved it into his pack.

"I'll clean her bowl," Cyrus replied. "You get started, and Knox and I will catch up."

Right. Because I was going to be painfully slow getting moving this morning. I scraped my bowl clean and handed it over to Cyrus, trying hard to not think about the fantasies I'd had about him while in that strange dream-state for the last few days.

I didn't know how long the images were going to be dancing in my head, but I sure hoped they would stop soon. I was already mated to Knox and soon to be mated to Bishop. I didn't need all three brothers. Two was more than enough.

And if I really thought about it. I should focus on figuring things out with my first mate before adding another one.

Bishop slung his pack over his shoulders, and with a groan, I staggered to my feet. The world lurched with the movement, and I clung to the boulder to steady myself, not to mention keep myself standing on my shaky legs.

What the hell had happened to me? Why was I so weak?

"If you're feeling up to it," Bishop said, sweeping me into his arms. "We'll get you walking for a bit after lunch."

"Yeah," I replied, grateful I wasn't expected to start hiking right away. Walking after lunch sounded like a good idea, although I had no idea if I'd feel stronger in a few hours or not.

Even just waking up, eating, and now standing seemed to have sapped all my strength.

"Weakness and exhaustion is a side effect of a heat fever," Bishop said. "It doesn't let you sleep or eat much until the fever is broken."

"And my fever only broke when Knox and I sealed the bond."

He'd said my heat had lasted nine days and I'd been unconscious or out of it for all of that. How many of those days had I been suffering with the fever? I doubt Knox would have jumped on the idea of sealing our bond right away. Hell, had they even known that was the only way to break the fever?

"Your fever went on longer than normal," Bishop said, answering my unspoken question as he quickly picked his way over the uneven ground. "We didn't know the mating bond was affecting the fever until it should have been over and wasn't. But it's done now and you're safe. I'm sure you'll be back to normal by the time we get to Stonehaven."

Given how weak I felt, I wasn't sure about that, especially since I didn't heal like a regular shifter. But that wasn't my greatest worry.

"So what now?" I asked, my voice frustratingly small.

Except that was how I felt. Small and weak and frustrated.

We'd suffered walking for ten days for nothing, and while I wanted to cry and yell at Knox and tell him how much he hurt me and how much it hurt that he didn't really want me — even though we didn't know each other — I was far too weak even at my strongest to make demands of an alpha. I was going to have to submit and accept whatever Knox decided.

A growl bubbled in my throat. I was tired of submitting, of trying to go unnoticed for fear of retribution.

"Now?" Bishop said. "I bond with you and we return home."

"Just like that?" I asked unable to keep my disappointment from my voice. We weren't going to bond because we were in love, but because we had to.

"Hey. I choose to bond with you because I want to, but if you aren't ready—"

"We don't really know each other and I—" My throat tightened. "I—" How could I say what I felt without sounding ungrateful?

"You wanted to be courted," Bishop finished for me as if he could see into my heart and knew how disappointed I was that he wasn't going to court me like he'd promised.

"Yeah," I confessed. "I never had a boyfriend. No one was ever interested in me and I never got... you know." God, it felt so selfish to say it.

"You never got the courtship gifts? The fancy dinners? The romance?" Bishop asked. He set me on my feet and cupped my cheeks in his palms to make me meet his gaze.

"You're allowed to ask for things," he said, his voice tender, his soft expression making my heart flutter with a mix of hope and fear. "Which would you like?"

"Well... I...?" I tried to look at my feet, my cheeks heating with embarrassment, but Bishop kept a firm grip on my face.

"You can say it," he urged. "You want all of it?"

"Yeah," I forced out. "I want to know what those first magical days of being in love feel like. I want to feel..." Like I mattered, like someone loved me for me not because an accidental bond was making them. And I felt like Bishop did, but I also felt like if we rushed our mating I'd miss out on all those romantic dreams and jump straight into the real life of being mates. "I want to feel like you want to mate with me because of me, not because you have to."

"I do, beautiful. I swear I do." He brushed his lips against mine, a whisper of a kiss that sent teasing sensual warmth sliding through my body. The kiss wasn't hungry with desire, not like his kisses when we'd first had sex or like the kisses floating around my foggy memory from my heat, but it still sent my heart soaring because it was a promise. A promise that I *did* deserve to be loved and that he'd prove it to me.

AUDREY

BISHOP CARRIED ME ALL DAY AS IF I DIDN'T WEIGH anything, only pausing when we stopped for lunch and for half an hour where I tried to walk on my own. And while I was feeling better, I was still shaky and weak, and it was obvious that my pace was a lot slower than the guys'.

Both Cyrus and Knox — once they'd caught up to us — stayed a good ten feet ahead of us. I doubted it had anything to do with wanting to offer us privacy since from that distance they could still easily hear our conversation with their better-than-human hearing, but I wasn't sure why they were giving us space.

Well, Knox, I knew was pointedly ignoring me because he still couldn't accept our bond, but I had no idea why Cyrus was.

Although maybe Cyrus wasn't outright ignoring me. He was just going about his business as usual. He hadn't paid that much attention to me when we'd walked north. It shouldn't surprise me that nothing changed on our way back south.

Except I couldn't shake the feeling that there was something more going on, something connected to my fever that I couldn't remember.

Also strange was the fact that Knox hadn't shifted.

Everyone had made it clear that he preferred his wolf form and he'd remained as a wolf for almost the entire walk to Kelna. I hadn't even known he and Bishop were identical twins until a few days ago... Well, I guess it was more than a few days now since I'd been unconscious for over a week. But it still felt like a few days to me.

We made camp as the sun was setting, the sky dark reds and oranges. Cyrus picked another campsite that was protected on three sides with rocky outcroppings, one of which had an overhang that would shelter us against the weather. We were about a hundred yards from a forest and the closest we'd ever set up camp to the river. If it hadn't been for the uneven ground and the bushes, I would have been able to see the fast-moving water from my seat near the overhang.

"Bishop, firewood. Knox and Audrey, fill the canteens," Cyrus said as he dropped the two packs he'd been carrying — mine and his — and yanked off his shirt.

"I can fill the canteens by myself," Knox replied. He dropped his packs — his and Bishop's — and unhooked the canteens.

"It's not far and she needs to rebuild her strength." Cyrus dropped his pants, exposing all of his powerful, muscular body, and my breath hitched.

The yearning from before didn't swell within me, I wasn't desperate for sex with anyone I could get ahold of, but I did warm up. I might not be in heat anymore or aching to seal my mating bond, but Cyrus was a handsome man — in a dangerous bad boy kind of way — and I was still a living, breathing woman.

"The water is moving too fast," Knox replied not bothering to look at the river. "If you want her up and walking, have her pace the campsite."

"The campsite is flat. The way to the river isn't and it'll be better for her," Cyrus said, a hint of his power rolling off him, the only indication his temper was rising.

"And *she* is standing right here," I shot back as I heaved myself to my feet and used the nearby rocks to keep my balance. "She's capable of making her own decisions."

"So, are you going to stay here or be useful?" Cyrus demanded, his words stinging, a reminder that I'd been a burden to him and his brothers since I'd stumbled into this realm.

"I'm going to help with the canteens." I might be weak, but I wasn't useless and I refused to let anyone take control of my life again. With the bond sealed, leaving was no longer an option, but I would prove to Cyrus and everyone else that I deserved the same respect as anyone in his pack.

Cyrus huffed, shifted into his massive black wolf, and bounded toward the forest to hunt for our dinner. Bishop shot me an encouraging smile and followed him.

"So…" I turned to Knox. This was the first time we'd been alone since we sealed the bond and a churning mix of emotions swept through me.

"You're staying," he growled, grabbing the other two canteens.

"I'll be fine. It's what? Fifty? Sixty feet to the river?" I shuffled a few steps toward the river, staying close to the outcroppings just in case I needed to catch my balance.

"I don't need your help." His gaze flickered to me then jerked away as if he couldn't stand looking at me.

"So, this is the way it's going to be?" I asked, unable to keep my grief and frustration from my voice.

If I was smart, I'd bottle it all away and not give him more ammunition to hurt me, but I'd always been terrible at keeping my emotions in. Sterling had seen through any front I'd put up and knew exactly where and how to strike.

I didn't want to go back to a life like that and yet sealing our bond hadn't seemed to change anything between us.

"It's the way it has to be," Knox replied.

"Why? I know this isn't what either of us wanted, but we're—" We were what? Going to have to figure something out? Make things work?

There wasn't a *we*, no matter what our bond said. And I'd never been able to *make* anyone do anything.

"Just mate with Bishop so we can move on," Knox growled.

"You mean so *you* can move on," I said, a new realization hitting me. "Is that what you're waiting for? Me to bond with Bishop so you can bond with someone else?"

The thought made my chest tight. I didn't want him to mate with anyone else. He was mine. But if I mated with Bishop it would only be fair. Maybe there was someone he loved and that was why he'd fought so hard against our bond.

Except I could feel the pull of the bond inside my chest, warm and comforting, locked around my heart, and knew even if we did bond with other people we wouldn't be able to move on from each other.

"Just bond with him," he snarled, not answering my question.

My chest squeezed tighter. He *did* have someone. I'd suffered for days feeling like I was going to shatter with all the ice he was shoving into our bond when he could have just said something at the start. I would have understood.

"It's what's best for you," he added.

"What's best for me?" Shock snapped through me. I couldn't believe he just said that.

Merrick used to say that as well, particularly when he'd first taken me in and I hadn't been as obedient and submissive as I should have been. He'd said Sterling hurting and belittling me was good for me. It would make me stronger.

But the second I showed an ounce of strength, I was punished, locked in the basement for a day without food, extra cleaning duties at his betas' houses on top of cleaning Merrick's, or forced to kneel in the snow or blazing sun for hours without moving, the alpha's power crushing me into submission.

It had never been anything that would leave a mark — although I had no idea why. No one in the pack would have challenged him if he had. But in some sick way, I think he actually believed what he was doing was best for me, and that made it even worse.

And now Knox was spewing the same shit. How dare he!

Anger burned in my veins, but instead of swallowing it back like Merrick had always demanded, I embraced it. Submitting had never saved me and I didn't care if it could save me now. How dare Knox try to crush me through a sacred bond and then tell me it was for my own good. Even if he was in love with someone else, that was no excuse for how he'd treated me.

"This has never been what's best for *me*," I snapped at him. "It's always been about you."

"We left our pack responsibilities to walk you to the death god's temple on the slim chance that we could break the bond. Don't tell me I didn't do this for you."

"Right," I said, my voice thick with sarcasm. "Because yelling at me that you didn't want me, rejecting the bond so thoroughly it felt like my soul was shattering, and being reminded every second of every day that I'm weak and worthless and no one wants me was all for me. You're so self-centered you think doing a favor for yourself is a favor for me. Well, fuck you!"

He tensed and his lips curled back in a snarl.

"What are you going to do? Punish me?" I demanded, opening my arms in invitation.

My frustration and fury screamed through my veins, hot and violent. It was so strong it felt like it was rolling off my body in waves and my pulse *thu-thudded* hard in my chest, powerful and ferocious.

"You can take your *best for me* and shove it up your ass, you selfish coward," I snarled. "If you hadn't wanted to walk for twenty fucking days you should have tried to figure something out, tried to come up with some kind of arrangement because this bond was permanent before you fucked me without my consent."

I jerked a step toward him, my body no longer shaking from weakness but from rage, a rage that made me feel powerful for once in my God damned life.

"You go fill the canteens by yourself and keep avoiding me. But this bond will pull us together whether you want it to or not, and I swear to God, now that my fucking heat is over, my strength of will is stronger than yours."

A low growl rumbled in Knox's chest and I jerked forward another step, the *thu-thud* inside me pounded louder, turning my fury into an inferno.

His eyes widened and something flashed across his expression too fast for me to recognize.

Yeah, he didn't expect me to advance, thought growling at me would scare me and make me retreat.

Well, fuck you!

Then he stomped up to me so close I had to strain my neck to look up at him. Power rolled off him in a crushing wave, stealing my breath, making my knees weak, and snapping electricity across my skin.

But I gritted my teeth and stood my ground. And I was going to stand my ground for as long as possible.

He could have had sweet, submissive Audrey if he'd actually made an effort, but now she was gone. She'd been hurt too deeply for too long and she'd had enough.

"You'll come begging to me," I said, my voice strained against the crush of his power. "You, the alpha, begging the weakest shifter in existence, and I'll make you wait. But don't worry. It'll be what's best for you."

His chest heaved and his breath rushed across my face in powerful, angry gusts. Our gazes locked — his with only just a hint of his wolf darkening his eyes even though I could see his anger — and I vowed I would *not* look away first. I would *not* submit to him.

Then his gaze flickered to my lips, sending a whisper of desire curling around my core.

Oh, no!

Oh, hell no!

I'd just told him I was stronger than him. I wasn't going to back down and I sure as hell wasn't going to let him kiss me, no matter what the mating bond wanted.

"No." I shoved him as hard as I could.

He stumbled back a step, moved only because I'd caught him off guard, and I pointed in the direction of the river.

"Go!" I commanded. My anger *thu-thudded* hard and fast, rolling off me in a great wave, and with a snarl, Knox stormed off.

I stomped around the sheltered campsite fuming. How dare he say it was best for me. How dare he!

Except telling him off had been stupid. We still had five maybe six days of traveling together and I knew once my adrenaline wore off, I'd regret screaming at him. I was going to have to live with him one way or another for the rest of my life. I couldn't escape him, and he was so much stronger than me.

But for right now, my body thrummed and I felt good. I felt powerful.

KNOX

Fᴜᴄᴋ.

I dropped the canteens on the rocks by the water's edge and strangled the scream threatening to rip from my throat. My cock was so hard it hurt, and I was furious and confused and grief stricken and—

Fuck! Fuck fuck fuck!

I grabbed a rock and shattered it against a boulder with my palm.

Audrey practically glowed with her fury and strength, a radiant, vengeful goddess, and I'd wanted to claim her all over again.

Except I also wanted to beat the shit out of myself.

If anyone else had hurt her as much as I had, I would have ripped their throat out.

Fuck. How had I not seen it? I knew she'd been struggling, knew freezing the bond hadn't been good for her or me, but that pain in her eyes when she was yelling at me crushed me.

I had done that to her in my fight to avoid trapping both of us in a bond that I now knew in my soul was fated.

I'd thought it had been her heat making her struggle, or at least part of it. I hadn't realized just how deeply my rejection had hurt her.

And now I had the gall to be pissed when she wouldn't even consider kissing me. I'd barely even thought the thought before she'd shoved me away.

What the fuck was wrong with me?

I shattered another stone and another, my throat tight from keeping my screams of frustration bottled in. But I was too close to our camp and I knew letting go would scare her.

I'd seen the fear of retribution in her eyes even as her temper got the better of her. I'd also seen the resignation, the acceptance that letting me know how she really felt would end in punishment. She was so angry with me, she was willing to face my fury.

She was so angry, I'd felt power, true alpha power like the power I'd felt in our shared dreams, rolling off her for just a moment.

It had rushed against my power, taunting, teasing, tempting, and my wolf had clawed and heaved against the collar. He wanted her just like how he'd had her in the dream, wanted that energy crackling against ours in a battle of dominance and seduction.

But she hadn't released her power in sexual challenge. Hell, she hadn't even knowingly released it, and I was sure she wasn't even aware she had it.

It had stuttered, the flow uneven, probably a match to the mix of rage and fear boiling over inside her, then it had flared sudden and strong, compelling me away from her, before vanishing.

I was worse than the asshole everyone thought I was. I'd hurt my mate so deeply the rage she kept locked within herself for fear of reprisal had burst free. She no longer cared if I punished her. Not that I ever would. But that didn't matter. I'd already done all the damage to our mating that I could.

I sagged to the ground, my smothered screams squeezing my chest until I couldn't breathe.

This was why I'd never be a good mate for her, why I'd fought so hard against the bond.

Except that was a lie.

I hadn't fought the bond because I thought I was terrible mate material. I'd fought it because I was afraid.

Fuck.

I had to fix this.

I just had no idea how.

I hadn't even known what to say to her when she'd been yelling at me. Normally I didn't care. I said what I thought and ignored and avoided those who didn't matter.

But Audrey mattered. She was the only one who mattered and, even if I had any idea what to say, being blunt wouldn't make her feel better and the thought of avoiding her forever made my soul scream.

She was right. She'd always been right.

The bond was inevitable and even if I stayed away from her, it would pull us back together.

I was a selfish asshole for not even considering that we'd have to figure out how our relationship would work. Even if she bonded with Bishop that wouldn't absolve me of my responsibilities to her and our bond.

I shoved a canteen into the river to fill it.

It had felt so good, so right carrying her while she was unconscious for those first few days after we left Kelna.

I'd been so sure I was going to have to let her go to embrace her relationship with Bishop that I'd clung to her every possible second until it looked like she was going to wake. But then I hadn't known how to say goodbye or deal with her sobbing, so I'd avoided her.

I couldn't have been a bigger idiot and now I needed to figure out how to fix it.

Except I had no idea how to fix a normal relationship let alone one as fucked up as the one I'd made with Audrey.

Hell, I didn't even know how to start one.

Movement downstream caught my attention and Cyrus pushed around a bush to get to the water's edge. He saw me and came closer to crouch a few feet away.

"I told Audrey to help you," he said, setting his catch — a skinned and gutted fox — on the rocks beside him, before shoving his bloody hands into the water.

"You should have minded your fucking business," I snarled. He'd made the order on purpose to force us together.

"And you should have taken the gift offered to you," he snarled back. "She's your mate and you've already fucked it up. She's shy and uncertain, but even a cornered mouse will bite back."

No shit. And she was hardly a mouse. She'd just been trained to act like one by the assholes who'd raised her.

"You don't deserve her," Cyrus said, his voice a low rumble, his wolf pushing to the surface. It almost sounded like Cyrus wanted Audrey as well even though he'd vowed to put the needs of the pack first.

"Then you do your fucking chores with her," I spat back, a sudden jealous rage surging inside me.

She was mine. Mine.

"I'm not the one who needs to build a relationship with her. You've avoided her from the start. Any idiot can see she doesn't trust you."

I huffed. She didn't trust me and she outright despised me.

And I deserved it all.

AUDREY

OVER THE NEXT TWO DAYS, I REGAINED MY STRENGTH enough to walk at the guys' pace for half the morning and ride Bishop in wolf form for most of the afternoon. I pointedly ignored Knox, and Cyrus didn't tell me to help him with his campsite jobs again. Instead, I helped Cyrus or Bishop — whoever wasn't hunting — with filling canteens, foraging for wild fruit and vegetables to supplement our meat, or gathering firewood.

The tension between Knox and I was palpable, and my fear of reprisal for yelling at him squeezed my insides, but I was determined not to back down. For once in my life, I was going to stand up for myself.

Knox had purposely hurt me and I couldn't just pretend to shrug that off. He could glower and avoid me or hell, even yell and hit me, but I had to stand firm. I couldn't run away from him like I'd wanted to run away from Merrick and Sterling, and I wouldn't go back to a life of always being afraid.

But God, it was so hard not to curl in on myself and try to make myself invisible.

"Tomorrow night we'll be camping just outside Darkweald," Bishop said as he helped me down a steep slope.

"At this pace, we'll probably reach the campsite by midafternoon," Cyrus replied, glancing up at the sun even though we'd just stopped for lunch half an hour ago, at noon. "We're making good time."

I bit back a sigh. Bishop had said our slower pace north hadn't been because I'd been walking and that we'd only made great time this time because the guys had pushed themselves while I was unconscious and when they were carrying me.

But I didn't really believe him. Yes, they looked a little more worn out than before, but I was pretty sure they'd have been able to handle the faster pace when we'd first headed out.

Except according to Bishop, they'd gone at the slightly slower pace — and he insisted it had only been *slightly* slower — because they'd thought we were going to be walking for the full twenty days. The rest at Kelna had been a welcome surprise... well, the rest that hadn't involved my body going crazy with a heat fever.

Cyrus skirted a copse of trees and hopped down another incline into a ravine that wound through the rocky landscape. I remembered it from when we were going the other way and it really did mean we were getting closer to Darkweald. Beyond the ravine lay a dense forest, then a more or less flat stretch of ground, and then the forest where the malicious god slept. We *were* almost home.

The thought sent mixed emotions swirling through me. I'd only spent a few days in Stonehaven and I already thought of it as home.

Except that wasn't entirely true. The guys referred to it as home so that's why I thought about it that way. Not because I had an emotional attachment to the place. Although I hoped I soon would.

I hoped the other pack members, if they couldn't accept me, would ignore me. That was probably the best outcome I could wish for and was a step up from my previous pack.

I stumbled down the second incline, falling into Bishop's arms, and flashed him a smile of thanks.

He'd been giving me longer and longer stints of walking and I was starting to feel stronger. Almost as strong as when I'd first started this journey.

"Want me to carry you?" he asked, his voice gruff.

"Half an hour more?" I asked, pulling out of his embrace.

"It'll be good for her," Cyrus called over his shoulder. "She's still too weak."

"I'll always be too weak for him," I mumbled, hopefully soft enough that he couldn't hear me. He was a good twenty feet ahead of us, so the odds were fifty-fifty.

"He pushes everyone," Bishop replied with a wry smile. "It's how he shows he cares."

He offered me his arm like a gentleman escorting a fine lady and I took it.

"You should have seen him after our mother and fathers died. He was an angry, growly, obnoxious beast," he said as we followed along the ravine after him.

"And if that's what gets you to combat practice and keeps you alive, so be it," Cyrus shot back.

A cloud swept over the sun, throwing us into shadows for a second. When it scuttled away, the sunlight caught in streaks of gold in Cyrus's light brown hair, streaks I hadn't noticed before.

The image of his eyes, filled with concern, his irises dark with his wolf's influence, swept through me. Then he dipped forward, wrapped his arms around me, and pulled me into a tight embrace as he plunged into me again and again and—

I shoved the fantasy aside even as a part of me questioned if it actually was a fantasy.

Had that actually happened?

Everything about my heat fever was so foggy and incomplete...

Which meant it was just another of my messed-up dreams. Just like the dreams I'd had of having sex with Knox, dreams that I hadn't had since we'd sealed our bond, or the shame dreams where a nasty voice called me names for what I'd done during the fever.

Cyrus wasn't interested in me, he'd made that clear,

and I was mated to his brother. That was the only reason he was being somewhat nice to me.

Another cloud covered the sun for a second and then another as a gust of wind swept down the ravine.

"We need to pick up the pace," Knox said from behind us.

I glanced back, unable to stop myself from looking at him even though I was determined to give him just as cold a shoulder as he was giving me. But he wasn't glaring at me for being too slow like I expected, he was glaring at the rapidly darkening sky.

"I remember there's a cave halfway down the ravine," I said as the first drops of rain splattered on the ground, darkening the rock.

"No," Cyrus replied, shooting down my suggestion without giving it any thought. "We need to go up. Get out of here."

I swept my gaze at the rocky walls on either side of us. They stood a good fifteen feet high and the bottom half was worn smooth.

Oh, shit.

Water smoothed rock meant the water in the ravine rose to above my head, and while we were in summer and could be standing in a dried riverbed, the more likely answer was that the ravine was a naturally occurring floodway during storms.

A heavy drop of rain plopped on my face and then another and another.

"I think there's a fallen chunk of rock a short way down," Bishop said.

Cyrus gave him a sharp nod and took off as Bishop scooped me into his arms and raced after him.

The fat drops quickly multiplied into a stinging, cold torrent, and the wind picked up with sharp bursts that stole my breath and made the guys stagger and fight against the force to keep moving.

I was drenched in seconds and forced to hide my face against Bishop's shoulder to keep the downpour from my face.

We reached the rock, an enormous chunk of stone that had broken off the ravine's side and slid to the bottom. Cyrus hopped up it with ease despite the blinding rain and turned back to us.

I'll get to the top and pull Audrey up, he said in my head, not bothering to yell over the roar of the storm.

Hurry it up, Knox shot back, his gaze on the steady stream of water running down the center of the ravine, now deep enough to cover his feet.

Bishop hefted me up as high as he could, and I scrambled the rest of the way up the rock to the top, while Cyrus jumped and grabbed the top of the ravine wall.

But just as he was about to haul himself up, a jackal leaped to the edge and snapped its sharp teeth at him.

My pulse jerked as he dropped back down and landed beside me, crowding me to the side and making my foot slip. With a yelp, I wind-milled my arms, fighting to keep my balance, knowing it was a losing battle even if the wind hadn't just gusted and pushed me over.

Fuck, Cyrus snarled and jerked forward, seizing my arm and yanking me up against his side, sending a flash of my fantasy rushing through my head.

But the heat vanished as quickly as it appeared. The rain picked up into a near-blinding torrent, the water level on the ground suddenly rising to Knox's ankles, and above us, half a dozen jackals stood at the edge, snarling and snapping blocking our only escape.

AUDREY

We need to make a path through the jackals, Cyrus said.

Toss training? Bishop asked.

Yep. See, showing up for combat practice is important. He turned his attention to me. *Bishop and I are going up first then Knox. He'll help you up. When you get up, run. Don't hesitate. Don't try and help. Just run. We can handle a bunch of jackals if we're not worrying about you.*

Because of course, I was a hindrance.

His words stung, but I couldn't deny them. I'd barely survived two fights with grimalkins, and while jackals were smaller, there was probably a whole pack of them just like the last time. And the last time Knox had been seriously injured to the point where shifting wouldn't immediately heal him.

I swiped rain out of my eyes and nodded. "I'll follow the ravine for as long as I can."

"Good girl," he praised, and he lowered me off the rock into Bishop's arms.

"Be careful," I told Bishop, squeezing him tight for a second. I didn't know what toss training was, but I knew climbing over the edge of the ravine would make him vulnerable and I couldn't bear the thought of losing him. Not when I'd just found him and things between us were filled with possibilities.

Bishop handed his pack to Knox then climbed onto the rock.

On three? he asked as Cyrus braced his back against the ravine wall and laced his fingers together.

On three, he replied.

Bishop placed his foot on the step Cyrus had created with hands, quickly counted down, and on three leaped as Cyrus propelled him into the air.

I rapidly blinked rain from my eyes, fighting the torrential downpour to keep watching.

With his incredible strength, Cyrus threw him into the air, the feat astounding since I doubted that Bishop, being almost as tall as his brother and packed with sculpted muscles, was lighter than the average man.

Bishop shifted in mid-air, the magic that let him shift destroying his clothes, and he landed on top of one of the jackals that was hanging over the ravine's edge snarling and snapping at us. With a growl, Bishop sank his teeth into the back of the beast's neck and wrenched his head, breaking its spine and killing it.

The other jackals lunged at him, but he bounded off

the jackal he'd just killed and tore out the throat of another one before the fight took him out of sight.

The jackals on the ravine's edge raced after him, their yips and snarls still loud, indicating that they hadn't gone very far. Despite that, Cyrus hopped up, grabbed the edge, and hauled himself up.

A jackal snapped at him, but he rolled out of the way — and out of sight — and a second later a dead jackal landed with a heavy, wet thump on the ground a few feet away... ground that was now almost completely covered in water, the gathering rain no longer contained within a narrow stream running down the center of the ravine.

Come on, Knox said, grabbing my hips and hoisting me three-quarters of the way up the rock in preparation of climbing out. *When I pull you up, remember to run.*

Right, I replied as I tried to scramble up, but my grip slipped on the wet rock and Knox had to set his hands under my ass to catch me. Then he shoved, boosting me high enough to get my chest over the top, and I dug my fingers into a narrow crack, scrambled for a decent foothold, and hauled myself up.

Gasping, I carefully stood and clung to the ravine wall to keep my balance and make room for Knox. The rain was now coming down so hard it was hard to see even a few feet in front of me and the gusting wind threatened to toss me off my precarious perch.

Knox easily climbed up beside me as if it wasn't pouring then jumped and grabbed the ravine's edge.

A jackal leaped at him, but Cyrus appeared, his

fingers extended into claws and his expression fierce, and he tore out the beast's throat before it could sink its teeth into Knox.

Get moving, Cyrus snarled as two more jackals raced toward him.

He caught the first one and tried to slash at the other as it raced past him, but it twisted out of the way, narrowly missing his claws. It dove at Knox who, already on his knees, ducked low, catching the beast's stomach against his shoulder, and tossed it over the edge.

The jackal landed on the ravine floor on its feet, only momentarily stunned from the fifteen-foot fall before jumping and snapping at me, trying to reach me on top of the rock.

Audrey, Knox barked, jerking my attention away from the snarling beast intent on eating me. *Grab my hand.*

He lay on his stomach and reached for me. Rain poured down his arm, splattering on the ravine wall and adding to the water stinging my eyes.

I reached for him, my fingertips barely brushing his. I wasn't tall enough.

Come on, he growled as I stood on my tiptoes.

More of our fingers brushed, but it still wasn't enough to get a proper grip.

You have to jump.

I dropped my gaze to the uneven, slippery rock beneath my feet. If I missed, I'd fall off and then have to figure out how to climb back up without help.

The jackal below me leaped again, his teeth snapping

close to my foot, making me jerk away. The movement threw my balance off and I clutched at the ravine wall, desperately holding on, praying I wouldn't fall.

Getting back up would be the least of my worries if I couldn't grab Knox's hand.

Audrey, please!

The desperation in Knox's voice snapped my attention back to him. Fear filled his expression, a look I'd never seen in his eyes before, and his gaze kept darting up the ravine and back to me.

What was he looking at?

I turned to look and time stuttered into slow motion. A massive wall of water rose at the far end of the ravine, roaring its way toward me.

I had to jump. Now. And I only got one attempt.

My pulse pounding, I leaped. Somehow my feet didn't slip out from under me, and Knox wrapped his large hand around my wrist.

But as he was hauling me up, the wave of water slammed into my legs.

I tried to hold on, tried to tighten my grip and futilely cling to the ravine wall, but the force of the impact yanked my hand from his.

Cold water engulfed me, the shock stealing my breath, and I was wrenched under. I fought to find the surface, but the current was too strong, tumbling me around and around.

Pain exploded through my head and sliced across my shoulder, and I belatedly realized I'd hit the ravine wall. I scrambled to find a handhold, but the water had already swept me away.

Another explosion of agony in my knee, my shoulder, my knee again, around and around. My lungs screamed for air and darkness swam across my vision. I flailed, fighting to find the surface or something to hold onto, but I could barely see what was around me and everything was moving too quickly.

AUDREY

THE WORLD HEAVED IN A WRITHING, FROTHING MASS OF dark water, and my lungs burned. What little breath I had was almost gone. Then something snagged my ankle, wrenching me against the torrent, and a strong arm wrapped around my chest.

Warmth billowed around my heart, strong and sure.

Knox.

Knox had jumped in after me... because of course if I died, he died or went insane. Not because he actually liked or was interested in me. Just like my nightmares had reminded me.

We crashed into the ravine wall, the impact shooting agony through my shoulder. Somehow he grabbed it with one hand and hauled us up enough for me to draw in a gasping, desperate breath before immediately coughing it and a whole bunch of water out.

Hold on tight, he snarled in my head, pulling me tight against his chest. *I need both hands.*

I wrapped my arms around his neck, hooked my ankles behind his back, and clung to him, my body trembling and exhausted and throbbing with pain.

With a growl, he dug his claws into the rock and hauled us up high enough that he could shove me over the edge.

Coughing and wheezing, I scrambled out of the water and collapsed on the hard ground, my body trembling from the effort, cold, and shock. The rain still pounded down in a painful torrent and the wind yanked on my wet hair and clothes.

Knox climbed up beside me, drew in a few deep breaths then picked me up, cradling me against his chest, and marched toward... I had no idea what. I could barely see anything more than dark mounds that, once we were close enough, turned out to be rocky outcroppings and boulders.

Somehow, he found us a sheltered crack that was barely wide and deep enough for the two of us if we huddled close together but would keep us out of the wind and rain. With a groan, he set me down and crouched in front of me.

"How badly are you hurt?" he asked, capturing my chin and turning my head to the side to look at what I could only assume was a cut at my temple.

My head throbbed, but it wasn't a migraine, and save for a pain in my knee whenever I twitched and my lungs still complaining about the water I'd breathed in, I didn't feel too bad. That and *I* wasn't the one in immediate danger. Bishop and Cyrus were.

"I'm fine." I tried to pull out of his grip but he held tight.

"You're not fine. You're bleeding and you almost drowned." He pressed a finger against my temple, sending pain shooting through my skull, and I sucked in a sharp breath that turned into hacking coughs.

"I'm fine enough," I choked out. "You have to go back and help Bishop and Cyrus."

"My brothers can take care of themselves," he replied, his voice gruff, and he turned his attention to the rip in my pants.

"It took all three of you to deal with the jackals last time," I insisted.

I didn't know how many there were this time, I hadn't gotten much of a look over the ravine's edge, but it seemed like every time Bishop or Cyrus killed one, two more had appeared. And while Knox hadn't needed an elixir for the last fight, he'd still been seriously hurt. If this new pack was bigger than the last, Bishop or Cyrus could be killed. It wouldn't matter if, as shifters, they were stronger than the jackals. There were only two of them and they were surrounded.

Knox made the rip in my pants bigger, revealing nothing more than a skinned knee.

"See? Fine. I can hide here and wait for all three of you to get back." They had to come back.

Fear tightened my chest. It was selfish, but I didn't want to lose Bishop. He was the first man to ever show any interest in me and a part of my soul wept at the thought of him dying... a part that felt far too similar to the part that was certain Knox was my mate.

"You have to go." My pulse *thu-thudded*, picking up speed.

"I'm not leaving you." Knox grabbed my arm and pulled me forward. Blood stained my shirt indicating that the cut on my shoulder that I couldn't feel was worse than my skinned knee. Still, It wasn't pouring down my body, so it couldn't be that bad. I'd survive. Bishop and Cyrus might not.

I wrenched out of his grip and shoved him back. "They're your brothers."

"And they're not my priority right now."

"Well, they are mine." My pulse *thu-thudded* again, harder, a pressure growing in my chest fueled by my worry.

Knox gritted his teeth. His power rolled off him, a great wave that stole my breath, but vanished a second later as if he'd changed his mind about forcing me to submit.

"Bishop is fine," he said, his voice gruff but not angry.

"You don't know that."

How could he be so calm?

He, Bishop, and Cyrus had been all about protecting each other and they'd made it clear they'd sacrifice me to

do so. I couldn't imagine the mating bond would drasti-
cally change Knox's priorities in such a short time.

"I'm not stupid enough to wander around by myself,"
I told him, "and I'm not bleeding to death."

"You hit your head. You need someone to keep you
awake and I still don't know how bad the cut on your
shoulder is." He held out his hands, silently asking for
me to show him. "And I do know Bishop is fine. If he was
seriously hurt, I'd feel it. Our twin bond is stronger than a
mating bond."

Stronger? What could be stronger than a bond that
deepened the love and soul connection between two
people?

If he knew when Bishop was seriously hurt, that
meant he could feel what Bishop was feeling, something I
couldn't do with Knox — and something I hoped he
couldn't do with me because if he knew what I was feeling, he was an even worse man than I thought he was.
That also meant Bishop could feel what Knox was feeling. Could he tell which were his feelings and which were
his brother's?

"No," Knox said, tugging me forward and ripping my
shirt a bit more to get a better look at my shoulder.

"No?"

"You're thinking Bishop only cares for you because of
our mating bond. That our twin bond is influencing
him," he said, taking off his shirt and ripping it into
strips. "It isn't."

"How do you know?" I knew I shouldn't have asked,

but I couldn't help myself. I wanted *real* love. Not love influenced by a bond I couldn't control.

"We've sealed our bond and the pressure is gone. The need to be with you isn't anywhere as powerful as it was before. If it had been influencing Bishop, his feelings for you would have changed. They haven't. Turn around."

I blinked at him, the order such a sudden change in the topic that I needed a second for it to register.

He motioned turning around with his finger and I turned, not worrying about whether I remained sheltered from the rain while I did so. I was already soaked and wasn't going to get dry anytime soon. Getting wetter now wouldn't matter.

"Bishop is still going to court you and I'm not going to stop him." He wrapped a strip of his shirt around my shoulder and another high around my chest.

"I'll also try with us," he said, his voice soft and gruff. "But I can't be a proper mate. That's why I was trying so hard to break our bond."

"You don't even know what I want in a mate."

"I'm barely a brother and I'm not a friend," he replied, pulling me into his arms, placing a folded-up strip of shirt against my bleeding temple, and inching us as deep into the crack as he could get so we were both out of the rain. "I doubt I can be a mate."

Heat from his body sank into me and warmth radiated around my heart. I wanted to argue with him about making assumptions and not bothering to talk to me, but I was too exhausted to fight.

I'd never been good at standing up for myself. It was always easier to give in. I still didn't want to let him off the hook for hurting me, but I could fight with him later.

Silence didn't necessarily mean submission, it just meant I was biding my time.

I huffed a soft laugh and leaned into his warmth, resting my cheek against his bare chest. Biding my time made it sound like I knew what I was doing when really I was groping around in the dark like I always did.

AUDREY

"Hey," Knox said, giving me a soft shake as the storm raged around us. "You're not supposed to fall asleep."

"Pretty sure that's a myth," I replied even as I forced my eyes open — eyes I hadn't realized I'd closed. "At least in my realm I think it's a myth. For all I know brains work differently in this realm, like hormones."

"I wouldn't know about that. I just know you're not falling asleep until sunset."

I looked out at the gloom unable to see more than a couple feet beyond our dry little crack. "Will we even know when it sets?"

"It'll get even darker," he replied dryly. "But I'm hoping the storm will pass soon."

"It did come on us suddenly." The sky had been bright with only a few clouds moments before the rain had started... or maybe I'd just missed the signs. We'd been in the ravine and hadn't been able to see the horizon. The storm still had to have been fast-moving since there hadn't been any cloud on the horizon when we'd entered the ravine just after lunch, but it might not have been as magically sudden as it felt.

Knox, however, didn't elaborate and I didn't want to pry answers out of him. I'd ask Bishop about it when he and Cyrus found us.

The rain continued to pour in a steady rush, picking up in pitch and volume every time the wind gusted. I watched a bush that was barely visible through the torrent thrash against a boulder. It jerked this way and that, unable to escape and forced to endure.

That was me now.

I couldn't escape Knox. I had to endure and make the best of my situation, but I also couldn't roll over and submit — like my screaming instincts insisted.

That would only lead to a lifetime of subservience and I was never going to go back to that. Ever.

It wouldn't matter if I also had Bishop as a mate. I couldn't let Knox think he could push me around again, even if he thought it was best for me.

But God! Just the thought of standing my ground again made my pulse race and my insides squirm.

"Bishop is still fine," Knox said, his tone still gruff, but his words surprisingly comforting.

Even if I hadn't been panicking about Bishop being in danger, Knox had sensed my worry and was trying to calm me.

"When do you think he and Cyrus will find us?" I

couldn't imagine them finding anything in this down-pour, but Knox had found this crack and they were real shifters who could see in low, to almost no, light.

"Tonight at the earliest," Knox replied. "The flash flood was moving quickly and we could have easily gone a few miles in a few moments. We were also swept past the slope where we would have exited the ravine and headed away from the river, which means we're past the split and they're going to have to find a way to cross it or wait for the water to go down."

The split was another ravine that joined the one we'd been following that had crossed our path. It had been easier to slide down the only available slope and follow the ravine leading north until we found another easy-to-climb slope farther along instead of trying to scale the almost sheer rock face on the other side.

"Do you think that other ravine flooded?" I asked.

"Probably."

Again, I waited for him to say more, creating an awkward silence between us, but he still didn't elaborate.

Swell.

"I guess that means we're even closer to Darkweald."

"We're in Darkweald."

"We're what?" I tried to jerk upright, but he tightened his grip, clutching me to his chest.

I couldn't believe the water had raced so quickly that we'd travel a whole day's worth of walking. But then I hadn't known how long I'd been in the water or where either ravine had gone to. I'd have thought they'd have both gone to the river, but the one had clearly branched away from it. Regardless—

"We have to get out of the forest," I said. There were dangerous spirits in Darkweald and from everything the guys had told me, they were most active at night. We had to leave before the sun set.

"Calm down," he snarled, a wave of his power rolling through me and making me go limp.

"Don't you dare!" I snapped at him, fighting his command.

"Then act reasonable."

"I am. The last time we were in Darkweald, flying snake monsters tried to kill us. If everything you guys have been telling me is true we need to get out of Tzanagoth's sphere of influence before sunset."

"I'm not dragging you back into the storm to hide for who-knows-how-long just to get out of Darkweald. It's bad enough you're bleeding and I can't make a fire to warm you up. Darkweald is a big forest and isn't all within Tzanagoth's influence. And even if we are within his influence, we'll be fine if we don't do anything to draw attention to ourselves."

"And you know this for a fact?" I demanded.

"I do."

Silence. Again.

Jeez. And I'd thought Cyrus was stingy with sharing information.

But as much as I wanted to know more, I sure as hell wasn't going to beg him for it. I couldn't escape — his grip around me was too tight — and even if I could, I didn't know where I was going and I could barely see. For all I knew, I'd stumble deeper into the forest.

We sat in a long, awkward silence until I couldn't keep my eyes open any longer and I let them slide shut. I wasn't completely recovered from my heat and I was exhausted, not to mention sore and my head was really starting to pound. The heat from Knox's body along with his smoky scent and the warmth around my heart from our shifter connection was too much and I soon fell asleep.

I woke with Knox's arms still wrapped around me and his warm breath gently caressing the side of my face. Sunlight streamed through a thin canopy of trees and that eerie stillness I'd felt the first time I'd stepped into Darkweald wrapped around me.

Knox hadn't lied. We'd been swept all the way into the forest... well, from the wide open area that lay beyond a few tree trunks in front of me, it was clear we were *just* inside the forest.

I wasn't sure how much time had passed, but it didn't look like it was close to sunset, and my gut told me the shadows were going in the wrong direction. Which meant it was the next day. Knox had let me sleep through the night despite what he'd told me about needing to stay awake, and there, about sixty feet away, were Bishop and Cyrus walking across the rocky ground toward us.

Relief flooded me. They were all right. Thank God they were all right.

"Thought you'd try to get ahead of us," Bishop said as he knelt in front of me and flashed me his panty-melting smile.

I tore myself out of Knox's grip and threw myself against Bishop's chest despite my body complaining from having slept cramped against my mate and what I was sure was a stunning collection of bruises from my watery trip down the ravine. I wrapped my arms around him, and he chuckled as he hugged me back, the sound melting the last of the frozen fear sitting heavy in my stomach.

"You're okay?" I asked, pressing my nose into the crook of his neck and inhaling his fresh-cut grass scent. Our shifter connection swelled around my heart and tears stung my eyes at how comforting it was. He was, and would always be, my soul's home.

"We're fine," he murmured, holding me tight before placing his hands on my shoulders and leaning back to look at me. "Better than you."

He brushed his fingers against my temple, sending pain spiking through my skull.

"It's just a few bruises and scratches." I shrugged, feeling every single bruise in that slight movement.

Cyrus huffed, drawing my attention to him. He was shirtless and his pants were ripped and bloody. Three red welts sliced across his chest, indicating just how deep the jackals' claws had cut into him that they couldn't be healed right away with a quick shift.

Bishop, on the other hand, looked fine. But then he'd

destroyed his clothes when he'd shifted and had to put on new, clean ones that hid any remaining evidence of the fight.

"She has a nasty bump on her head, a deep cut on her shoulder, and a skinned knee," Knox told him. "Little more than a few bruises and scratches."

"Not enough for an elixir," Cyrus replied. "Come on. We're on the eastern-most side of Darkweald, about as far as we can get from the patrol shed and not the three-quarter day hike we would have had if we'd camped where we were supposed to."

Aaaand somehow our change of camping location had become my fault.

Jeez. I couldn't win with Cyrus. Not that it mattered. He wasn't my mate and wasn't interested in becoming my mate like Bishop was. He was just my brother-in-law and my pack alpha. Someone I was going to be connected to for the rest of my life.

AUDREY

CYRUS LED US DEEPER INTO DARKWEALD, FOLLOWING WHAT looked like a game trail — and at times no trail at all — and we passed through the forest without incident.

We also, thankfully, avoided Anakar, the temple complex where I'd first arrived in the realm. I didn't want another run in with Sterling or Royce since they'd already proven they didn't need to be in the same realm as me to control me and threaten my life, and I didn't need another reminder.

And while it would have been nice to know the rip between this realm and mine was gone, I was sure someone would report what was going on with it some-time soon to Cyrus. I could ask him about it later.

We walked all day and reached the patrol shed just after the sun had set. It surprised me that there was no one around. If they were investigating the rip, the shed was the most logical place to make camp. It had a well for clean water, was guaranteed shelter against the elements and any beasts in the area, and was out of Tzanagoth's influence where his spirits couldn't reach them.

Of course, if the rip was closed, there'd be nothing left to study and everyone would have returned to Stone-haven. Either that, or after the flying snake spirit incident, they decided it was too dangerous to stick around.

Cyrus and Bishop got to work building a campfire with the wood piled against the side of the shed, while Knox, much to my surprise, took my Cyrus-assigned duty for the night and filled up the water bucket.

I didn't argue like I would have, like a part of me screamed I had to so I could prove I wasn't worthless. I might have shrugged off my near-death experience in the ravine when talking with Bishop, but my aches had only gotten worse the longer we'd walked, and I was grateful for Knox helping me with anything. I also didn't have high hopes I'd feel better tomorrow.

Tomorrow night, however, I'd sleep in a real bed, be able to have a real shower, and not have to walk any great distance ever again. Hopefully the day after tomorrow, or the day after that, I get back to feeling like myself.

Just one more day to go and this whole, horrible ordeal would be over.

Except it wouldn't be because I was now permanently mate bonded with Knox.

I bit back a sigh, wrapped my thin blanket around me, and snuggled closer to Bishop. One more day and then, good or bad, the rest of my life would begin.

The next morning, Knox took my pack without saying anything, and he and Cyrus led the way back to Stonehaven. I stayed about fifty feet behind them with Bishop even though my heat was over and I no longer needed to keep my distance from them.

"I can't decide if I want to spend a week soaking in a bath or sleeping," I said as I finished my lunch of more dried rations and heaved myself to my feet.

Bishop chuckled. "You could do both, but I don't recommend it without supervision."

I glanced at him, but his back was turned to me and I couldn't tell if he was being literal and serious or flirting with me.

It had to be flirting, right?

"Is that an offer?" I asked, my voice suddenly husky and my cheeks burning with the embarrassed fear that I was wrong.

"Absolutely," he replied, flashing me a smile that made my pulse stall for a breathtaking moment. But then his smile quickly faded. "We're going to have to wait a few days for that though. Even with Nova and Deacon running things, work will still have piled up." His gaze jumped to Knox who was already on the road headed to Stonehaven.

My mate hadn't said anything to me today, but I hadn't gotten the sense he was avoiding me or angry with me like he'd been for most of our journey. It felt more like he didn't know what to say. And while I could sympathize with him, I wasn't going to let him off the hook.

I'd vowed I wouldn't break first and I wasn't going to. No matter how uncomfortable it felt to make an alpha apologize to me.

"I'm going to be busy for the next few days, maybe a week," Bishop added. "But you should take it easy and stay close to the Residence. You've been through an ordeal. You deserve time to recover."

"Yeah." Sour disappointment oozed through me and I pushed it back. Bishop wasn't brushing me off. He was saying he just needed time to take care of pack business.

Besides, I had my relationship with Knox that I had to figure out, along with what I was going to do with the rest of my life. If Cyrus was also busy with pack stuff and didn't demand I make myself useful right away, I could take a few days to decide some things. Things like if I wanted to stay in the Residence, what job I wanted to do, and what I needed to do to become literate — since the magic of this realm let me speak and understand their language but didn't let me read it.

I didn't like the idea of being all on my own, especially when some of Cyrus's and Bishop's betas didn't like me, but I doubted they'd do anything to outright hurt me. This wasn't my old pack after all. If I kept to myself and didn't draw anyone's attention, I'd be fine.

I huffed a bitter laugh.

That plan hadn't worked with my last pack. Was I foolish enough to think it would work with this one?

"But I'll still see you at dinner every night," Bishop continued, his words reigniting the warmth around my heart from our shifter connection even though he wasn't holding me. "Even if you weren't Knox's mate, you'd be welcome at dinner."

Yeah, I thought to myself. I *was* foolish enough to hope everything would work out. I might even be right this time.

Stonehaven came into sight just after dinnertime, and I took in the buildings sprawling down the mountainside, those closest looking like modern buildings and those farther away surrounded by a thick, Medieval-looking stone wall.

If I pretended the older buildings didn't exist, I could have been back home in Oregon. At least until I tilted my gaze up and looked at the two moons, one that looked like the regular moon and one smaller and pinker, reminding me I wasn't in my realm.

As much as I was grateful to be here with an alpha who wanted to protect me and not own me, I still had a lot of confusing emotions about not being on Earth. Emotions that I'd been ignoring because they were insignificant compared to everything else that was going on.

And in reality, even though I was now more or less safe, and my mate bond with Knox had been dealt with — even if the outcome had been disappointing — how I felt about being in this new realm still didn't matter. I couldn't do anything about it and wouldn't go back to Sterling and Royce even if I could.

Although if those two psychopaths weren't a part of the equation, would I feel differently?

There were things I really missed from my realm, like cars and coffee, and my realm had so many things that I wanted to show Bishop. He'd been excited to learn that I'd seen a real angel. How would he react to TV or cell phones? The internet would probably blow his mind.

Hunh.

I didn't know exactly how most things worked, but I knew of things that didn't exist in this world. Perhaps with Whil and some of the pack's inventors and engineers I could share some of humanity's ingenuity and they could figure out an equivalent for their realm. There wasn't electricity here — that I knew of — and I wasn't going to introduce them to fossil fuels, but they had a lot more magic than my realm did. It was literally sleeping in the ground around us.

Maybe I wasn't so useless.

Once Bishop had taken care of his piled-up work, I'd talk to him about sharing what I knew.

Cyrus and Knox — who was still, much to my surprise, in his human form — left the road before we'd made the final turn and crested the last hill to reach the town.

I raised my eyebrows at Bishop once they were out of earshot and he just shrugged.

"Pack business," he said. "We've been gone long enough that once word gets out that we've returned, we might get swarmed, and there are few things they need to take care of before that happens."

I shrugged back. I didn't know what that could possibly be, but then I'd never been an alpha or privy to any of my previous alpha's business.

I pondered Bishop's words as we walked the rest of the way, doing the math on how long it had actually been. When I woke from my heat, the guys had said there were five days left to reach Stonehaven, and yep, we'd walked for five days.

Before that, I'd been unconscious for three days of walking and nine days with my heat. That was seventeen days just to get home, plus the ten it took us to get to the death god's temple.

My pulse lurched. I'd been traveling for almost a month.

I'd been in this realm for a whole month.

Which meant my birthday was in a month. I'd turn twenty-three, and my wolf would still be asleep. If I even had a wolf.

My shock at having been in this realm for a month along with all my fears and uncertainties soured the thought of my upcoming birthday. Not that birthdays had ever been a time for celebration. They were always a reminder that I was lacking, and Merrick and Sterling made sure I was aware of that.

Of course, since I'd only had Mila and no other friends or family, it hadn't really mattered if I'd been able to celebrate my birthday or not.

But shockingly, a part of me had hoped that being away from my old pack this year might be different, that there might be a few people who'd want to help me celebrate the way I'd seen everyone else celebrate.

I glanced at Bishop through my lashes, wondering if I should tell him? Were birthdays something celebrated in this realm? Did I want to draw attention to myself like that?

AUDREY

I was still flipflopping between telling Bishop about my birthday and hoping for some kind of celebration or keeping my mouth shut so I wouldn't be disappointed when we reached the first building at the outskirts of town.

A lanky man about my age, maybe a little younger, stepped out of the shadows, stopping us.

"You're back!" he gasped. Then his wide green eyes swept around us and narrowed with worry. "Where are Cyrus and Knox?"

"They're fine," Bishop assured him. "Taking care of some business before the betas swarm us. Are you our welcome party?"

"Sort of. Deacon set up extra watches since there was a grimalkin attack and told us to keep an eye out for you. You've been gone so long, I was starting to get worried, but now you're back," he replied. "Did you find what you were looking for?"

I shot a glance at Bishop. I didn't know how to answer that and wasn't the wolf in charge. It wasn't my place to say anything.

Bishop shook his head. "Unfortunately, no."

"Well, that sucks." The young man huffed, his gaze jumping to me, his expression brightening. "At least you look better than the last time I saw you," he said as he held out his hand. "I'm Zavier."

I reached to shake it, but Bishop released a low, dangerous growl along with a snap of power, and I jerked my hand back, my pulse pounding. It had been years since I'd heard it, but Merrick used to growl like that. Just before he'd punish me.

I didn't know what I'd done wrong, but it had to be something about shaking Zavier's hand, which reminded me that I couldn't assume things in this realm were the same as mine. For all I knew, I was now off limits for every other man because I was mate bonded.

Except that didn't make sense, especially since the guys had told me they'd have sent me to the heat clinic to have sex with strangers which was a lot more intimate than shaking someone's hand.

Zavier's eyebrows jumped up beneath the hair flopping over his forehead, showing he was just as surprised by Bishop's reaction as I was. Then his gaze dropped to his feet and he took a step back. "Forgive me, alpha. I didn't realize—"

"No," Bishop said, his power vanishing. "Forgive me. It's been a difficult few weeks."

"I mean there's gossip about Cyrus and the outsider, but I—" Zavier began. "I mean I thought— But of course you both can—" His face turned bright red and I didn't know if I should laugh or cry.

If Zavier was a gossip, everyone was going to know before tomorrow morning that Bishop was interested in me. Which was true, but I didn't know how public he wanted to be about us, especially if it came out that I was also Knox's mate.

Except that shouldn't be a problem because he'd already told me that monogamy wasn't a requirement for wolves in this realm.

Cyrus on the other hand was going to be pissed that people were still talking about an *us* that didn't exist. We'd been gone almost a month and whatever he'd said before we'd left hadn't been enough to squash the rumors.

"The outsider's name is Audrey," Bishop replied, saving Zavier from any more incomplete sentences. "And she's no longer an outsider. She's pack." He placed a possessive hand on my shoulder and a whisper of power slipped his control.

Zavier bobbed his head and shifted back another step. "Understood, alpha. Welcome to the Stonehaven pack, Audrey."

His tone was overly formal, and his gaze focused on my right ear as if I were an alpha and he didn't want to make eye contact and challenge me.

Swell. I could see other members of the pack being pissed that a shifter who couldn't even shift was being treated like an alpha. I could only pray that Zavier wasn't a gossip and he wouldn't tell everyone how he thought they should behave around me.

I also prayed that Bishop got ahold of himself. I didn't even know what had set him off. It wasn't like Zavier had been rude to me.

Two guys a few feet up the street spotted Bishop and waved. He nodded in response, placed a hand on my lower back, and urged me forward up the busy main street and away from Zavier and the awkwardness.

More people looked at us and nodded, smiled, or waved but thankfully didn't approach. I was too tired and sore to put on a brave face around strangers and was suddenly uncertain about where I stood with Bishop.

"So, ah... What was that about?" I asked once we were far enough away from Zavier. I tried to keep my voice steady but couldn't help the sliver of fear creeping into it. Bishop had seemed so relaxed and kind, and I'd never seen him throw his alpha power around like that.

Of course, that was a reminder that I barely knew him. I'd only been in Stonehaven a few days before it had just been the four of us walking through the wilderness. For all I knew, he had all the undesirable alpha traits and I just hadn't seen them yet.

"Sorry," he mumbled as he palmed the back of his

neck and looked sheepish. "He was checking you out and I just got... angry."

Angry? I bit the inside of my cheek to stay silent. It was best to keep my mouth shut. Looking embarrassed for overreacting was the behavior I'd expect from Bishop. But being angry for no reason wasn't like him. I'd been in that conversation, too, and Zavier hadn't been checking me out. Who'd want to check out someone like me? That kind of response was more like Knox.

My pulse stuttered.

"Could your twin bond be influencing you?" I asked, my voice frustratingly small because if it was the twin bond, that could mean no matter what Knox had said about Bishop's feelings for me, they weren't real. They were just from my mating bond with Knox.

"Probably," Bishop said with a sigh, making my throat tighten.

What he felt for me wasn't real.

"Hey, no." He tugged me to the side of the road, hooked his thumb under my chin, and tipped my head up, forcing me to look at him. "Not like that. What I feel for you is all me. It has nothing to do with my connection with Knox. He's stressed right now and he expresses that with anger which sometimes puts me on edge." His expression softened and he huffed a soft laugh. "I never expected it'd make me possessive."

"Never been jealous, hunh?" I tentatively teased.

"Oh, I've been jealous about a lot of things, like how Cyrus always seems to have it together, or how Knox is the best hunter in the pack and I'm not even in the top twenty." He flashed me a wry smile and offered me the crook of his elbow. "But I've never been jealous over a woman. What she does is always her choice and only my business if it involves me."

I hooked my arm around his and let him continue to escort me up the main road. "So, I can shake hands with any guy I want?"

"You can do more than shake hands." He rumbled again, the sound low and soft in his chest, and he released another sigh. "My wolf would prefer if you just stuck with shaking hands."

So, he wouldn't control me, but his wolf, the most primal part of his being, wanted me for himself. Or at least, himself and his brother... brothers?

The thought sent warmth rushing through me. His wolf wanting to control what I did should have bothered me, but instead it sent a thrill rushing through me. He *wanted* me. No one had ever wanted me, and I trusted that Bishop had enough control of his wolf that he wouldn't let him abuse our relationship.

"So, no conversations?" I asked, more confident in my teasing. "What about brief eye contact? Should I avoid other women as well?"

"All of the above," he said with overexaggerated seriousness. "I decree that only blind, mute servants shall attend to you and everyone will have to wear blindfolds when you wish to walk about the town."

"Everyone, hunh?" I laughed with him. "That seems dangerous."

"Seriously, though. Even if Knox is around, you can do and say what you want with whoever you want. You don't belong to him or me or anyone."

I squeezed his arm in thanks. "There might still be some social rules that I don't know about and inevitably mess up," I replied, turning serious. "You behave like everyone back home — better even — and I understand your language and you don't have an accent. Sometimes I forget this is a different realm and a different culture. I don't know what I don't know, and you don't know it, either, so you can't help me avoid it."

"That's a lot of *don't knows*." He bumped my shoulder with his, drawing my gaze up to see the warmth and affection in his brown eyes. "It'll be all right. You're not alone anymore, Audrey. You've got me." His wry expression deepened, his eyes sparkling with laughter. "And believe it or not, you've got Knox. His social skills suck, but for what it's worth, he won't betray you."

Because the bond wouldn't let him.

But that thought didn't ring true. Knox was harsh and gruff and might not like me for putting us in an unwinnable situation, but I knew in my soul he'd never purposely be cruel. Not like Sterling had been for all of my teen years and not like Royce when he'd tricked me into thinking we were fated mates.

"Speaking of having your back," Bishop said as we passed through the open, unguarded gate in the thick stone Old Town wall. "We all agreed that you can't keep staying in the guest room."

"So where will I be staying?" After the conversation we just had, I didn't think they were going to throw me out of the alpha's residence to fend for myself, but I did fear that they were going to move me in with Knox, something I wasn't at all ready for.

"A guest suite. You need more space to call your own to figure out what you want to do. Something a little less temporary. The suite has a bathroom, bedroom, and a sitting room."

"I'm pretty sure I can think just fine in the bedroom you've already given me," I instinctively replied, years of declining big *gifts* that were really traps having taught me to say no to everything. No matter how much I wanted it, it was always safer to turn it down even if that meant being reprimanded for being ungrateful.

"It's already been decided. By now Cyrus has already had someone move your clothes."

Clothes that they'd also bought me.

"I can't keep taking advantage of your good will."

"You're not just pack now. You're family," Bishop said. "Hopefully soon you'll be family twice over when you accept me as a mate as well."

My pulse fluttered in anticipation of the thought, even as a whisper of fear curled in my stomach. I wanted so desperately to believe him, believe everything was as it looked to be, but I couldn't kill that sliver of worry that I was wrong and I was going to go back to living in a nightmare.

We reached the gate in the stone wall surrounding the Residence and passed through. Beyond, the Residence was highlighted by a band of sunlight streaming between two mountain peaks as if the realm were putting the building on display. And it was worthy of display, looking like a spectacular, enormous Medieval castle with multiple turrets and wings and a grand front door.

"You belong in the Residence with your mate," Bishop said.

But that was only if my relationship with Knox had been normal, if I'd actually been chosen. At the moment, I was his dirty little secret.

My throat tightened at the thought. "Is he going to acknowledge me?"

The muscles in Bishop's jaw flexed.

That was a no.

"It's okay," I replied, even though he hadn't actually said anything, the sting of being rejected yet again making my eyes burn with tears I didn't want to cry. "Our mating wasn't because either of us wanted it. Best not to let the pack think there's more between us than there actually is."

"He doesn't want the mating to create trouble for you until the pack knows you. He'd never willingly mate with someone, so there's going to be questions."

"Not ever?"

Bishop shrugged as we entered the Residence, stepping into the grand front entrance with its enormous glittering chandelier, thick red carpet, and sweeping staircase. The staircase started with stairs on either side of the entranceway then joined halfway up to create a grand archway over the doorway to a large ballroom before splitting again and leading to the wings on either side of the building.

My room had been up the stairs, to the left, and a few doors down, but instead of taking the stairs, Bishop led me down the righthand ground-floor hall and along a series of other halls.

"I'd like to think he would have found someone on his own eventually, but I know I was just fooling myself. He'd been withdrawing more and more, not coming back to us like we hoped," he said, and I could tell there was more behind his words than he was saying. Knox had left them for some reason and it didn't sound as if he'd willingly returned. "But then you came, and I've seen more glimpses of my real brother than I ever did before... well... everything. It's not your place to heal him and I don't expect you to, but just being in his life has helped."

We stopped at a wooden door carved with sweeping scrollwork and a shiny silver doorknob. It was much fancier than the door of my previous room.

"Audrey," Bishop said, his voice low, sending a shiver of attraction slipping down my spine.

I raised my gaze to meet his and fell into his warm brown eyes, mesmerized by the bright green flecks. God, he was so beautiful and kind. I had no idea how I'd gotten so lucky that I'd just fallen into his life and he accepted me. If someone else had found me, my time in this realm could have been very different.

The memory of him pushing into me as I begged for more more more rushed through me along with a wave of heated embarrassment.

After what had happened, it could have been really awkward between us, but while I still felt flashes of embarrassment, Bishop had never made me feel uncomfortable.

"I'm glad you came to us." His gaze dipped to my lips and my pulse fluttered with anticipation.

We hadn't done more than cuddle since my heat. I hadn't felt as if I was ready for more and he hadn't brought it up, somehow just knowing I needed space.

But now my insides were warm, the heat sinking lower and lower, and the embarrassing memories were also exciting.

"I'm glad you came to *me*," he said, his voice husky, sending shivers of anticipation racing down my spine.

AUDREY

MY PULSE POUNDING, HALF IN FEAR OF REJECTION AND HALF in hope, I rose onto my toes and brushed my lips against Bishop's. It was a test to see if the connection I felt between us was still there after my heat and not my imagination.

A rumble rattled in his chest again, the vibration somehow hotter and more sensual than his angry growl, fueling my confidence.

He felt it, too, the need, the yearning. The attraction was still as strong as ever and with a soft moan, I tangled my fingers in his hair and tugged him closer so I could deepen our kiss.

Without hesitation, he dipped in and captured the back of my waist with his arm to steady me but let me stay in control of the kiss until both of our breaths came too fast and my body was hot and tingly.

Then he took over, pinning me against the door and

plundering my mouth with a desire that stole my breath and left no doubt about his intentions.

"Audrey," he groaned as he jerked away and pressed his forehead to mine. "If I didn't have to check in with my betas—" He brushed his thumb over my cheek then took a jerky step back. "What just happened here, between us — It's a promise for more to come."

My pulse throbbed, my body aching with the need for more but I nodded instead and didn't press for more. Desire and disappointment warred inside me, but strangely no sadness. He wasn't rejecting me. He was saying 'not right now.'

And God! I couldn't wait for him to fulfill that promise, couldn't wait to be with him again when I was conscious enough to enjoy it.

"Take a bath and relax. I'll have dinner brought to your room." He cupped my cheek, his attention on my lips as if he were going to kiss me again before pulling even farther away. "Sleep as long as you like. You deserve it, and there's no need for you to be on any kind of schedule until you've decided your future."

He quickly strode away as if walking too slowly or looking back would break his willpower.

I watched him go until he stepped out of sight, then sighed and opened the door to my new room.

Inside was an opulent room done in creams, tans, and browns with gold accents. A large fireplace sat against the lefthand wall with a mantle covered in scrollwork that matched the door.

In fact, everything was covered in matching scroll-work: the couch and matching chairs' wooden frames, the dark wood four-person dining room table with its matching chairs, and everything else that could be ornamented. It had to have taken a craftsman months, possibly even years to complete such detailed and extensive work.

The plush couch and chairs faced the fireplace, creating a conversation area, while the table sat at the back and to my right, leaving room for the French doors — which I doubted were called French doors in this realm — that led onto a small patio made private by a flowering hedge and planter boxes.

The room was easily three times the size of the bedroom I'd originally been in, and I hadn't even stepped into my new bedroom or attached bathroom.

That thought sent a mix of pleasure and discomfort rushing through me. I liked the idea that Bishop wanted to pamper me, but I also felt like I was drawing attention to myself, and being noticed was dangerous.

My new bedroom was just as opulent as the sitting room with a large canopy bed, the mattress big enough that it would have been considered extra king size in my realm, a full-length mirror that could show two people standing side-by-side, and a large wardrobe.

It sent more mixed palpitations rushing through me. When Bishop had said I needed more space, I hadn't expected it to also come with an upgrade to first class.

My few pieces of clothing had been hung in the

wardrobe, barely taking up any space, and I vowed *I* would be the one to fill it. Not Bishop. I needed to start doing things on my own. I *wanted* to.

And now I could. Here, in this new realm, I was my own person and I'd been given a second chance. I didn't want to let it go to waste by becoming dependent on Bishop. I wasn't afraid of hard work, and I was sure I could find a way to earn my place in this pack in a way that wasn't just as Knox's and Bishop's mate.

The bathroom was similar to the one I'd used before — except this one was private, not shared with the other rooms in the hall. It had shiny chrome fixtures and white marble everything: floors, counters, and tiles. A tub, larger than the previous one, sat at the back, looking just as welcoming even though it didn't sit in a bay window overlooking a garden, and the stand-up, glassed-in shower was also larger, big enough for three people.

Just like the other bathroom, it was fully stocked, and I turned on the water to fill the tub and dropped in some bath salts that smelled fruity and sweet.

With a groan, I pulled off my boots and peeled away my filthy shirt and pants. My skin was mottled with scratches and bruises from being swept away in the flash-flood, and I was so dirty, I felt as if I should peel my skin off, too, and throw it on the floor with my clothes. I really didn't want to get in the bath while covered in filth. That would just be gross.

New plan!

I slowed the stream of water filling the tub, hopped

into the shower, and scrubbed away all the grime that had built up from having walked for almost a month with only two showers and a handful of cold dunks in the river.

By the time I'd scrubbed down and washed my hair twice, the tub was full, and I sank into its sweet-smelling warm embrace and let my mind go blank.

But as I sat there half staring at the marble tiles and half drifting off, an uneasiness grew in my chest. The weight slowly getting heavier and heavier, twisting into something cold and sour.

I shifted, hoping a change of position would relax me, but the uneasiness continued to grow.

It had to be the room. That was the only thing that had really changed in the last little while. It couldn't have been returning to Stonehaven. I hadn't felt like this for the few days I was here before we left for the death god's temple.

No. It had to be the new *suite*. It was too much, too luxurious. Someone like me wasn't given a room like this without it being a trick or a mistake and I felt like it was going to be ripped away any second and I was going to be banished to the basement. Or rather, since this was a castle, the dungeon.

Did Cyrus even know Bishop had moved me to a suite? Bishop had said they'd all agreed, but upgrading someone with almost no useful skills didn't seem Cyrus's style. I didn't deserve a room like this. I barely deserved the room I'd originally been given.

Except that was something Merrick and Sterling would tell me, and Bishop wasn't like them. Cyrus and Knox weren't like them, either. They might not have welcomed me or thought highly of me, but they hadn't tricked or punished me.

Yet, a small voice whispered inside me, even as my heart and soul assured me it would never happen. The mating bond might let Knox reject me and be angry with me, but it would never let him be purposefully cruel.

And while Cyrus was tough and didn't sugarcoat things, he didn't strike me as cruel either. Without a doubt, all of them would eventually do things to hurt me, but their intent would never be malicious.

Which meant I just had to get over myself and accept the fact that someone wanted to do something nice for me with no strings attached.

Really.

Except the sense of unease didn't diminish with my certainty that the guys weren't screwing with me. It was going to take a while to let go of all the doubts and fears Merrick had driven into me for far too many years, and telling myself things were different wasn't what would help. I needed proof. I needed Bishop and Knox and Cyrus to keep treating me differently until it finally sunk in. My own words to myself didn't matter.

And neither did soaking in the bath.

I was still too worked up. I could spend all day in the warm water and it still wasn't going to relax me.

With a sigh, I climbed out of the tub, dried off, and

wrapped myself in the big, fluffy robe hanging on the hook behind the door.

While I'd been in the bath, someone had entered my suite and set a large silver tray with my dinner on the table in the living room. That only added to my unease. I didn't like that anyone could just come and go from my suite. I should have thought to lock the door, but I'd been distracted by Bishop's kiss on top of being tired from our long journey.

Had that been Bishop's intent? To distract me?

No. Just no!

I couldn't start doubting him. He'd taken care of me and been kind and sweet for the entire journey. I had to break the cycle of mistrust and doubt.

But the unease kept growing, twisting in my chest, making me twitchy.

What the hell was wrong with me?

I hadn't been afraid like this in the entire time we'd been traveling and there'd been times when I'd be in serious danger.

But my current fear wasn't because my life was being threatened. It was the fear that the safety and comfort I felt with these men in this realm wasn't real, that it was all a trick, just like my mating bond with Royce.

I paced the room, hoping movement would burn away the tightness that was slowly squeezing my chest, but it didn't help. I picked at my meal, a pasta in cream sauce with a side salad but couldn't bring myself to eat much despite having been ecstatic about not eating camp food when I'd first returned to the city.

Jeez.

I collapsed on the bed and buried my face in a pillow. Sleep — if I could fall asleep — was my last option before I broke down and ran screaming through the halls.

With a groan, I rolled over and pressed my hands against my chest. It was so tight now that it was hard to breathe, my unease blossoming into full anxiety.

I could only pray sleep would reset my brain and I'd no longer be freaking out in the morning.

AUDREY

A LOW, MENACING CHUCKLE WHISPERED OVER ME, AND I wrenched around, searching for whoever was laughing, my pulse racing.

Once again, I stood in my old pack's sacred grove, surrounded by undulating red mist. And while logically I knew being back on earth was impossible and I had to be dreaming, the rest of me was too afraid to care. The monster was coming and this time it would eat me.

I bolted into the thick underbrush, running like I had that horrible night, barely able to see in the darkness. I didn't care when the shrub and tree branches sliced at my skin or I bashed my shins or bare toes against rocks, I ran as hard and as fast as I could. I had to get away. I couldn't get caught.

Lightning lit the forest around me, a shocking burst of light that passed too quickly for me to tell where I was before plunging me back into darkness. A second later, the menacing laugh returned, now a rolling thunder and part of the storm closing in on me.

"You can't escape," a voice hissed.

"I can. I did," I yelled back, fighting to be heard over another roll of thunderous laughter. "I'm in a different realm. You can't get me."

Ahead, a hint of soft light glowed through the thick branches and my pulse leaped with hope. The way out of the forest and this nightmare.

With a growl of determination, I picked up my pace, shoving through a dense bush with sharp thorns, and ran back into the sacred grove.

No.

I twisted to look behind me. The bush I'd pushed through was gone and had become the familiar path between the two towering oaks that the pack used to enter the grove.

How did I get back here?

It was easy to get lost and turned around in the forest, but I couldn't have run in a wide circle. Not without hitting a recognizable landmark first. And the bush I pushed through. It had just disappeared.

Because it's a dream, my logical voice cried, barely audible against another burst of thunder.

"It's because you can't escape me," Sterling replied, his voice echoing around me, sending shivers of fear rushing down my spine.

"You can't escape *us.*" Royce stepped out of the darkness, his expression filled with the same worry he'd had when he'd tricked me into starting the mating vows despite his ominous words.

"I did escape you," I insisted even as my body took a step toward him.

"You can't escape fate." He held out his arms and my body stepped into his embrace, despite my mind screaming at me to run the other way. *Now. Run now!* "You belong to me."

He tugged me closer and captured my lips in the same scorching kiss from before. It was just as powerful and overwhelming, but instead of igniting a dizzy desire, it ignited fear. Now I knew the truth, knew that what I'd felt had all been a manipulation of magic, a trap I'd blindly jumped headlong into.

"No," I gasped against his lips, trying to shove him away. "I refuted you. I don't belong to you."

"You said the vow," he sneered, his fingers tangling in my hair and painfully jerking my head back, exposing my neck. "You practically threw yourself at me, so desperate for someone to love you."

"No."

"Yes." With a growl, he nipped my lips with wolf-sharpened teeth, drawing blood and a flicker of pain, tighten his grip around my waist, and ground his hard length against my belly. "You bound your soul to mine, Audrey. You belong to me."

"That's not true. I'm bound to Knox." Even before Knox and I had sealed the bond, I'd known I was bound to him. I felt nothing for Royce and I never would.

Royce shoved his hand down the front of my dress and roughly palmed my breast as his teeth grazed over my collarbone.

"You could fuck their whole pack, but you'd still be mine." He pushed the top of my dress down and sucked on my nipple with a force that shot a gut-churning mix of pain and desire to my core.

"I don't want you. I never wanted you." I shoved at his head, trying to get him away from me, but he sucked harder, and the pain turned into liquid need. It burned through me like the feverish heat I'd just survived and my knees buckled.

"You do want me." He tightened his grip in my hair and bit down hard on the flesh about my nipple, his sharp canines drawing blood.

More pain sliced through me and my core clenched in anticipation.

"No." No no no.

This wasn't me. I didn't want him. He was manipulating me just like he'd manipulated me that horrible night.

I heaved in his grip. He was a psychopath. I couldn't be attracted to a psychopath. I couldn't be bound to one.

And I wasn't.

I was *not*.

Because this was some sick nightmare, all my worst fears coming true, and I couldn't make myself wake up or break free.

"Stop," I begged, tears blurring my vision. I clawed at

his face and hands, anything to get away from him, but my nails just skidded over his skin, not even drawing lines on his flesh. "I'm bonded with Knox. Not you."

"But you're a greedy cunt," he sneered. "You want his brothers, too. You want anyone. You want me."

"I don't want you!" I screamed, slamming my fist as hard as I could against his temple.

With a roar, he shoved me and my knees slammed onto the hard ground. I scrambled away from him, my body screaming in pain, my transformation dress ripped down the front and my chest bleeding from Royce's claws just like that horrible night.

"I'll never want you. You're a monster!"

"But I have you." His lips curled back in a vicious smile and tendrils of black smoke lashed around my body, seizing my arms and legs and pinning me to the ground.

The inky tendrils raced around my waist digging into my skin and pinching my nipples, but — thank God — my body didn't heat with desire and betray me this time. Only pain and fear roared through me, making me tremble and tightening my chest until I could barely breathe.

"I'll never be yours," I gasped, heaving and snarling, determined to be free, despite the panic roaring through me. "If I ever see you again, I'll kill you."

Royce threw his head back and howled with laughter. "You won't even be able to touch me."

The tendrils oozed up my neck and started to tighten.

"I will," I gasped, heaving and thrashing. "I'll kill you." I wrenched one hand free and clawed at the smoke, tearing into it as if I had claws, the wildness from my dreams with Knox rising up within me, giving me a crazy, manic strength.

"I'll never be yours," I screamed. "I'll kill you!"

AUDREY

I JERKED AWAKE, MY PULSE RACING, MY BODY STICKY WITH sweat and ugly red scratches up and down my arms and around my neck from where the sticky black smoke had captured me in my dream. The unease sat tight and heavy in my chest, worse than before I went to bed, and tears rolled down my cheeks.

Furious, I wiped them away. I was done with him, done with all of them. They couldn't reach me and I was finally safe.

I. Was. Safe.

God, why couldn't I make myself believe that?

I dragged my bleary gaze to the window, the curtains still open since I'd collapsed on the bed and hadn't bothered to shut them.

Dawn was just starting to lighten the sky, which meant I'd slept for most of the night, but I didn't feel like it. I was still exhausted, and the unease still seethed inside me and made me tremble.

With a groan of frustration, I got out of bed and slipped into a dark blue, backless dress with a high neckline that hid the scratches at my throat and was made from a material thick enough that it wouldn't show off my nipples. Not that I had to worry about being perpetually turned on now that my heat was over.

Normally I would have preferred a shirt and pair of pants, but for some reason I balked at the idea. I wanted to look pretty just in case I came across Bishop, and he'd spent the last month watching me get dirtier and dirtier in a shirt and pants. I didn't want to remind him of that. I wanted to remind him of the woman in the pretty dress he'd made love to the night of the wedding in Kelna.

Trying to remind myself that I likely wouldn't see Bishop until dinner and that I shouldn't get my hopes up, I headed down the quiet halls to the kitchen.

Inside, two women — one middle-aged and the other about my age — were making morning pastries. The young woman sang and danced as she worked while the old woman was more restrained and just hummed along with her. They were still in the early stages of their work with the young woman filling a pan with what looked like cinnamon rolls and the older one working on a batter that I guessed was intended for the empty muffin tray on the counter beside her.

Breakfast clearly wasn't ready, but I suspected if I asked, there'd be fruit and bread in the fridge.

Except, even though I hadn't eaten a lot last night, I wasn't hungry. The unease was like a vise around my chest, making it hard to breathe, and it fed an angry irritation that was sure to get me in trouble if I talked to anyone.

And since I still wasn't entirely sure where I stood with Cyrus and the pack, I didn't want to risk pissing off the wrong person. In my old pack, the wrong person had been everyone except my friend Mila. I had to assume until I knew otherwise that it was the same here.

Which meant it was best to step away before one of them saw me.

And here I was being terrified of reprisal from everyone once again.

The thought made me want to scream and I hurried out the front door, hoping that being outside would help.

But the crisp air and the peaceful early morning silence did nothing to diminish the unease and frustration and anger — so much anger — boiling inside me.

Jeez. What was wrong with me?

I'd never been so angry in my life.

But maybe it was about time. I'd barely stood up for myself when I was a child and Merrick had punished that away within a year of living with him. Now I was free from him and his son. Perhaps all the rage and fear I'd kept bottled up all the years had finally broken free.

If that was the case, I needed to figure out how to get rid of it before I yelled at the wrong person. Just because

I was Knox's mate and Bishop was romantically interested in me, didn't mean I had immunity from bad behavior.

Sure, shifters tended to be more volatile in nature than other supers, but losing it for no apparent reason was still bad.

I marched around the Residence's grounds. My emotions roiled inside me and my thoughts were a jumble, searching for a reason for why I'd finally broken. Then my thoughts jumped to my horrible childhood then to the terrifying moment when that monster had started to eat Merrick while he'd still been alive then back to the beginning again. Around and around and around I went.

It wasn't fair.

It just God damned wasn't fair.

And while logically I knew life wasn't fair, I couldn't get my emotions under control. All that blood, all of my *father's* blood, splattering the bathtub tiles, all the punishments, all the fear about when Sterling would attack next, building and building until I couldn't breathe. All the hope Royce had given me in the blink of an eye before crushing it completely.

How dare they! How dare all of them.

I'd been trapped in my life through my naivety and my position in my pack, and I was still trapped. I was trapped in my bond with Knox and I was trapped in my own body, my wolf form locked away forever.

A ferocious wildness rose inside me, and I threw my

head back and screamed, desperate to release the pressure crushing my chest.

Tears of heartache and frustration and emotions I couldn't even recognize streamed down my cheeks. I could be brave for Bishop, and I could hold out until Knox apologized for hurting me, but I was always going to be broken. Always.

The sudden need to escape crashed over me. It consumed every other thought and feeling, propelling me into a wild run out the Residence's gates, through Old Town's narrow winding streets, and out into the newer part of Stonehaven. I ran and ran and ran as if I could run away from the hurt and fear and shame inside me.

As if I could run away from who I was and become someone else.

I ran until I was straining for breath, covered in sweat, and my whole body trembled from exertion, and then I sagged against an alley wall damp with morning dew.

The wildness still churned inside me, desperate to escape, furious at being trapped, the emotions so strong they felt like they belonged to someone else. Weak little Audrey would never feel anything so deeply. She'd never scream and run like a mad woman.

But maybe that was what I was now. A mad woman. Maybe I'd finally lost it, my soul broken, just like my father's. Just like my nightmares had whispered to me.

I raked my hands through my hair, pushing it away from my face, and sucked in deep breaths, determined to steady myself.

Each inhalation hurt my chest, the pressure and unease still clawing inside me, and the urge to run still made me twitch, but both sensations started feeling foreign as if they weren't mine as if they belonged to—

Knox.

My pulse stuttered. The need to escape and the blinding white rage were Knox's emotions, and they were fueling my own insecurities.

Something was happening with him, something that was making him feel so strongly he was influencing my emotions through our mating bond.

I pressed my hands over my chest as if that would somehow focus my connection on our bond. I needed to distance myself from him and regain control. It was bad enough he could physically control me with his alpha power. Now he could make me feel things I wasn't really feeling through our bond.

But the second I thought that, I knew he wasn't doing it on purpose. He was in trouble and the only way to stop the onslaught of unwanted emotions was to help him. Now. Now now now.

Except I had no idea where he was.

Hell, I didn't even know where *I* was.

I hurried out of the alley and looked down the street. From the street's width and the large stone paving tiles, as well as the smaller brick on the two- and three-story buildings on either side, I had to be in a newer part of town.

I didn't recognize any of the buildings and from

where I stood I couldn't see the Old Town wall. There were about a dozen people on the street. Most were carrying bags and heading somewhere — off to work maybe? — while a few were setting out sandwich boards and turning on lights in the nearby stores.

From the angle of the shadows and the mountains looming to my right, I guessed I was facing southeast, and since I couldn't see Old Town, that meant it was behind me. But when I turned to head the other way and return to the Residence, the pressure of Knox's emotions surged, stealing my breath and filling me with a desperate urgency.

I jerked back to the southeast and the pressure turned into a sharp pull, yanking me forward a few steps before I realized what I was doing.

I hadn't been running blindly through town. Knox's emotions were pulling me to him... because he needed me. Whether he knew it or not, his overwhelming emotions were a call for help. One that, even if I wanted to, I couldn't deny.

I took off, letting the pull lead me down the street. The path drew up close to the mountainside before opening into an enormous courtyard blocked in by the mountain and two-story buildings on either side.

Pillars had been carved into the side of the mountain framing half a dozen large openings and the pull led me through the closest one into a dimly lit hall. The pressure surged again and I ran down the hall, faster and faster. The rage that had consumed me earlier threatened to take over and I knew if I didn't get to Knox soon, I'd lose myself to it again.

Knox was inside and the sense of urgency squeezed tighter.

I bolted down the hall. Large faintly glowing stones placed every twenty feet along the wall at head-height offered barely enough illumination for me to see with my practically-human vision, but it was enough to keep from tripping and to spot the tunnel leading deeper into the mountain.

This way. Hurry. Hurry. Run. Fight. Kill.

More light, brighter than what was in the hall, shone from the end of the tunnel, and I raced toward it, straight to a closed metal gate.

Shit.

I grabbed the cold bars and heaved, but the gate wouldn't budge. It was locked.

No! I had to keep going. It was the only way to stop the emotional onslaught before it took over again.

Beyond the gate lay an arena lit well enough to see everything in the center, but not so bright it was blinding. It had been built in an enormous cavern in the heart of the mountain and had a polished stone floor, a wall about a foot taller than me surrounding the "field," and two dozen rows of bench seating surrounding it.

Knox, in his wolf form, prowled the arena floor, snarling and baring his teeth. Pools of blood darkened the floor with a ripped piece of clothing lying in the center of the largest one. He looked as if he were a real wolf trapped in a cage and not a shifter, his movements jerky and wild.

I pressed a hand against my chest, clinging to the gate with my other hand to keep standing, and focused on the pressure inside me. This close to Knox, the pull felt like it was tearing my soul from my chest, and a rage and primal wildness that needed to rip everything apart threatened to seize me.

I wrenched my eyes open and strained to suck in a steadying breath. The emotions coming through the bond had exploded into a vortex that tore at my insides and likely tore at his as well.

For whatever reason, the primal core of his wolf was devouring the human half of his soul, and if it succeeded, I'd lose my mate forever.

I had to get in there. I had to save him.

The lock on the gate required a key that I didn't have, so I swept my gaze around, looking for it or a way up to the arena's seating, anything that would help.

There. About ten feet behind me. A passage I hadn't noticed because I'd been focused on the gate and the light beyond it.

I rushed into the passage, up the short set of stairs into the first row of benches, and climbed over the edge of the wall determined to get into the arena as fast as possible. If I hung from my fingertips, the fall was only a foot or two, but the stone was smooth and I'd barely gotten turned around and over the edge, when my fingers slipped and I crashed to the arena floor, landing on my butt.

A low growl jerked my attention up and I locked gazes with Knox as he bolted toward me with no glimmer of recognition in his eyes.

My pulse stuttered.

He wouldn't hurt me. I was his mate. If I died, he died. But did his animal half understand that? He was so angry, so determined to kill everything.

"Audrey!"

A wave of power crashed over me along with the sudden need to run away. I wrenched my gaze around the arena, searching for a way to escape even as a part of me screamed that the impetus came from someone's alpha power, not me.

On the far side, Cyrus and Deacon leaped over the wall to the arena floor their expressions filled with panic and raced toward me.

Both guys looked like they'd already fought with a feral wolf and barely escaped with their lives, and if all the unease churning inside me came from Knox then that meant they'd been fighting with him since last night.

How had it gotten so bad? And why hadn't they shifted out their injuries? Unless, of course, they were bad enough they feared the shift would exhaust them and they wouldn't be able to keep doing whatever they were doing with Knox.

Cyrus, who still wore the pants he'd worn yesterday morning indicating that he and Knox had gone straight to this arena when we'd returned to Stonehaven, had lost his shirt and held one arm against his stomach. Blood smeared his chest and ran from beneath his arm and down his legs, soaking into his pants, while Deacon's whole right side was bloody. He held his right arm to his chest, blood leaking from long gashes that ran from his shoulder to his elbow.

Behind them, Bishop lay on a bench, not moving, and my pulse lurched with a new fear. I couldn't see if he was injured, but I also couldn't see if he was breathing.

Oh, God! Had Knox done that?

"Run!" Cyrus roared at me and another burst of power made my muscles tense.

But there wasn't anywhere to go and the command only added to the emotions crushing my chest. I couldn't climb back up the wall. It was too tall. The closest gate was locked. And there was no way in hell I'd be able to outrun a wolf.

And now I was no longer certain that Knox wouldn't hurt me.

He'd mauled Cyrus and hurt Bishop and they were his brothers. I was just some weak little girl who'd forced a mating bond on him.

AUDREY

"Knox, stop!" Cyrus yelled when he realized commanding me to escape wasn't working.

An enormous wave of power slammed into me, Cyrus willing to freeze me in place to control his brother, and I dropped to my knees before I could even think of doing anything else.

But Knox kept running straight for me, his eyes wild and his teeth bared, Cyrus's power not affecting him.

"I. Said. Stop." The pressure of Cyrus's power increased, and darkness swept across my vision, narrowing it down to a pinprick where I was focused on the massive black wolf barreling toward me.

"Knox," I gasped, his name a whisper on my lips as he crashed into me.

God. This was it. He was going to kill me.

The impact knocked me onto my back, and he pinned

me down with his front paws and clamped his teeth around my throat.

My pulse *thu-thudded*, straining against Knox's physical and emotional weight along with the weight of Cyrus's power that crashed again and again, stronger and stronger, with his desperate attempts to control Knox.

But Knox didn't move, didn't even raise his head to look at his brother, who was clearly more of a threat than me. His hot wet breath huffed against my throat and he released a low growl.

Mine, his wolf snarled in my head, his voice filled with rage.

Black specks danced across my vision and I fought to breathe even as my body shook with fear. With a snap of his jaw, Knox could kill me.

Mine mine mine. Knox's wolf released my throat and jerked his attention to Cyrus and Deacon, stopping them a good sixty feet away from us with a low, dangerous growl. *Mine.*

He looked ready to attack, his teeth bared, his body tense.

Mine.

"Let her go, Knox." Cyrus took another step closer, his claws extending from his fingertips, and the muscles in Knox's back legs bunched.

He was going to attack, and while Cyrus and Deacon were two of the most powerful shifters I'd ever met, they were already bleeding. A lot. I didn't want to think about the damage Knox's wolf would do if he thought they were trying to take what was his.

Bishop had said wolves in this realm weren't possessive, but I wasn't sure that applied to Knox, or at least Knox's wolf.

Mine, he roared again, adding a suffocating wave of his own alpha power to the already suffocating mix.

"I am," I gasped, praying that he wanted to protect and not hurt me and cupping his furry cheek with a trembling hand.

The touch drew his attention away from his brother and Deacon and back to me, and his dark eyes, filled with vibrant green flecks, captured me, stealing my breath and flooding me with his emotions: rage, fear, yearning... hurt.

I didn't know why he hurt, but I recognized that he, too, was broken in ways others didn't see or understand. I also felt his acceptance, or what had been his acceptance of how he thought he was before I'd come along, and the agony that he wasn't worthy of having a mate.

I bit back a bitter laugh. *I* was the one who wasn't worthy in our relationship. I couldn't even shift.

He growled, his wolf pushing back his human emotions and insecurities and replacing them with a blinding fury. Those emotions would never get in the way again, not so long as his wolf was in control.

But that wasn't good for him or me or anyone. The wolf half of a shifter's soul was his primal half. It didn't understand complex emotions or the need to sometimes sacrifice those emotions to protect someone.

Like protecting a girl who didn't know he was broken.

The realization of what had happened hit me, and I brushed both hands into his thick fur, urging him to keep looking at me. He hadn't taken his wolf form since before I'd had sex with Bishop, a form I'd been told — and had seen for myself — that he preferred. Which meant he'd been actively suppressing his wolf.

If his wolf was determined to keep me as a mate, then it would have taken everything he had to keep that half of his soul from taking over while I'd been suffering through my heat. He might have even had to collar his wolf to keep him contained.

And now his wolf was pissed, had taken over, and was never letting go of their body.

"I *am* yours," I repeated, praying his wolf could sense my sincerity. "But I'm also his."

I wouldn't be able to have a relationship with him without his human form, and while his wolf might even be strong enough to shift into a human, we still wouldn't be able to connect in a way only our human souls could connect.

He huffed, his dismissal of his human half clear in that snort.

"He hurt both of us," I said, "but you know it was to protect me."

Out of the corner of my eyes, I saw Cyrus creeping closer. I needed to hurry and convince Knox's wolf to let me go and agree to the natural balance found in all shifters' souls. Because if Cyrus attacked, Knox's wolf was going to go completely feral and do something he wouldn't be able to come back from, like kill his brother.

"You know he did it because he was afraid."

He'd said he'd done it for my own good, but now I knew it wasn't because I was weak, but because he thought he was broken beyond repair.

Maybe he was.

But maybe so was I.

That didn't mean we could avoid what fate had forced on us.

"You know it in your heart." I slid my fingers through his soft fur, keeping my movements slow and soothing. "You know he thought he was doing the right thing for me."

He huffed again, the sound softer and some of the tension eased from his body.

"I'll always be yours. I need you to show me how to be strong. But I also need him. He's as much my mate as you are. Can you let him go? Please?"

Mine, he rumbled, but all the rage and possessiveness were gone. In its place were love and wonder and a little bit of hurt, not because I'd hurt him for asking for human Knox back, but because Knox had forced him away and resisted what his wolf had known was fate.

Whether we liked or even knew each other, accidentally mate bonding with him hadn't been a mistake. We were fated mates. Neither of us could deny it.

Audrey? Knox, the human, gasped in my head, and the churning unease that had been squeezing my insides since last night vanished.

The green flecks in his wolf's eyes brightened for a second before he collapsed on top of me, his body shifting from his heavy wolf to his almost equally heavy human form.

"What the hell are you doing here?" Cyrus roared as he stormed toward me. His rage rolled off him in waves of uncontained power, making my pulse race and my mind whirl.

"What?" I didn't understand why he was so mad. I expected him to be relieved that I'd brought Knox back.

But he was furious with a rage I'd never seen before, one that reminded me too much of Merrick and Sterling.

"Did you follow Bishop, thinking because he's interested in you the rules don't apply to you?" he accused.

"No." I shrunk back from him, instinct screaming that I make myself smaller and hide because I couldn't get away. "I just—"

"You just what?" He rolled Knox off me, fully exposing me to his furious glare. "Deacon, take Knox to the grove before he wakes up here and freaks out," he commanded without looking away from me.

Deacon dropped his kilt, shifted from human to wolf and back again, turning the gashes in his arm into not-as-bad but still bleeding cuts, then resecured his kilt. He shot me a concerned look as he hefted Knox onto his shoulder, except I couldn't tell if he was worried for me or concerned that I was what Cyrus was accusing me of: someone who thought the rules didn't apply to her.

"We don't know how long he'll be out," Cyrus said with a snap of power. Then he frowned and Deacon raised an eyebrow as if he expected an answer.

The muscles in Cyrus's jaw flexed, his fury sinking into a simmering rage, and Deacon nodded. The beta's expression was still concerned, but he obviously wasn't concerned about me because he turned on his heel and carried Knox out of the arena, leaving me alone with Cyrus and his now partially contained fury.

I curled in on myself, my arms wrapped around my stomach, trembling at the thought of what was going to happen now and trying to be as small as possible. Even if Cyrus had pulled in his temper that didn't mean anything.

"You just what?" he repeated, his voice low and dangerous.

"I—" I squeaked.

No, damn it. I didn't want to be small. I wanted to be strong.

"I felt—" I said, struggling to sound more confident.

I tried to scramble to my feet, but only got halfway up before the force of Cyrus's wrath pushed me to my knees and consumed that flicker of determination that had told me to stand in the hope that he'd gotten his emotions under control.

But this was just like what had happened with Merrick in those early years. There'd been times when he'd calmed down for a moment, usually when there was a witness, but as soon as the witness was gone...

It didn't matter if I had a good reason or not for jumping in and saving Knox, I knew what came next. The alpha was always right and always punished those who disobeyed him.

I was a fool to think I was anything other than what I was.

I clenched my jaw, fighting the urge to look down, and failed, my gaze dropping to the polished stone floor in submission. As much as I wanted to be strong, to be someone new in this realm, and as much as I'd momentarily lost my mind and tried to goad Knox into punishing me for talking back to him. I was weak and I'd always be weak.

"You can't go sneaking around. Ever. It's dangerous. Knox could have killed you and we would have lost both of you. You," he growled, his tone growing darker with each word, his control vanishing. "You are not exempt from the rules. You might be mated to one of the pack alphas but you are *not* an alpha. You can't just do what you want whenever you want."

"Yes, alpha," I forced out, hugging myself, desperate to stop shaking. "I'll learn my place, alpha."

Remember your lessons, I told myself, my throat tightening and my eyes burning with tears. *Stay calm. Stay small.*

Cyrus growled, the sound a precursor to violence, and I squeezed my eyes shut. I couldn't let him see me cry.

Crying was weak. Crying wasn't submitting to the will of my alpha and accepting my situation.

Just stay small. He'll do whatever he'll do and then it will be over.

Until the next time.

He threw his head back and roared, the sound echoing through the arena, and I flinched, anticipating a strike.

But instead of hitting me or ordering a punishment, he stormed away.

Tears rolled down my cheeks and I fought to stay silent. I couldn't let him hear me. I couldn't risk bringing him back.

For whatever reason, he hadn't vented his anger on me and I needed to keep it that way. He was so much stronger than Merrick or Sterling, both in alpha power and physical strength. He could easily hurt or even kill me. I didn't stand a chance against him.

God! I didn't know what had happened. I didn't understand how Cyrus could turn on me so quickly, but maybe I'd been wrong about him. Traveling together had been extenuating circumstances and this was what he was really like when he was leading his pack.

Except that didn't match with how he'd been at dinner with his betas and how they'd all been comfortable joking and disagreeing with him.

But none of that really mattered. I'd forgotten myself. I'd let my guard down because I'd thought I was safe when my whole life was proof that I was never going to be safe. Bishop had seemed sincere in his promise to court and mate me, but that didn't mean I was safe from Cyrus.

A sob broke through and I slapped my hands over my mouth to muffle the ones that were sure to follow.

I'd really thought things were different, but I was even more trapped here than I was in my old pack. The only thing I could do was keep my head down and make myself as small and as invisible as possible.

CYRUS

WITH BISHOP'S UNCONSCIOUS FORM OVER MY SHOULDER, I stormed away from Audrey as fast as I could before I did something stupid like grab her, drag her up to my bedroom, and lock her inside so I always knew where she was and she was never in danger again. I'd never been so furious and so terrified in my life.

She'd fallen into the arena and Knox, little more than a feral wolf at that point, had charged her.

My heart had completely stopped and I was certain he was going to kill her.

If he'd been completely feral and he'd killed her, he wouldn't have died or gone insane because of their broken mating bond.

How the hell had she even found us? She had to have followed Bishop after he'd shown her to her new rooms... which didn't explain why she'd waited until the morning to jump in or didn't come running when Knox was trying to kill us or react when Bishop's last attempt to use his twin bond with Knox had knocked him out.

Sisters! Knox had been going crazy all night, slipping further and further into feralness, and had attacked us as if he hadn't recognized us. We'd been trying to pin him down long enough for Bishop to calm him and use their twin bond to bring him back like he'd done the last time, but Knox was more ferocious than I'd ever seen him.

Deacon had almost lost an arm and I'd almost had my stomach ripped open. We'd been unable to shift to heal ourselves, since Knox would have seen that as an act of aggression, and none of us wanted to leave the others alone in the arena to go outside. That and I wasn't sure if shifting would fully heal us. It certainly wouldn't have left us with enough strength to battle Knox.

Then Audrey had shown up, naive and vulnerable like she always was. It didn't matter that he hadn't hurt her, that she'd been exactly what he'd needed to regain his humanity. She. Could. Have. Died.

I didn't know how to get that through to her. I hadn't meant to yell at her, not like I had with my power raging out of control.

Deacon had even warned me to calm down — thankfully through a telepathic link because embarrassing me in front of her would have completely set my wolf off — but I couldn't calm down.

If she'd just stayed where she was supposed to, she wouldn't have been in danger. I needed her to understand that, understand that seeing her in danger, seeing her die would turn *me* feral.

But she hadn't heard what I was trying to tell her. She'd shut down, shrinking in on herself, staring at the floor, and trembling, which only made me angrier. Angry that her immediate response was to become fully submissive. I knew she had more fight in her than that, I'd seen it during our journey to the death god's temple.

Except whatever fight she'd been born with had been trained out of her. The shivering, small woman who'd just cowered in front of me was what her previous alpha had made her.

And now she thought I was the same as that monster.

I bit back a howl but wasn't strong enough to fully contain the wave of power rolling off me. I needed to get away from her, from everyone, and calm the fuck down.

I didn't want her to look at me like she was terrified ever again.

And yet... maybe it was for the best. If she hated me, there couldn't be anything between us.

Because there *couldn't* be anything between us.

And I couldn't stop thinking about her.

The memory of pushing into her tight, slick heat and holding her small soft body was burned into my brain.

I wanted more than a fevered desperation that she didn't fully remember. I wanted the smiles and heated looks she'd given Bishop after her first time with him. I wanted to protect her, lift her up, and show her she could do anything.

I wanted her.

But the pack might not see what I saw. They'd see a shifter who couldn't shift and I wasn't going to risk putting her through that. Mating Knox and Bishop would be what was best for her, and I needed to forget all about her.

Hell, she didn't even remember having sex with me. I suspected what she did remember she thought was just a fevered dream, which was why she kept glancing at me, looking confused and blushing, and a part of me prayed she'd always believe it was just a dream.

It was the coward's way out and I hated being a coward, but she'd cried for days while partially sedated and still blushed when she looked at all three of us. Knowing we'd all seen her naked and begging and that we'd all slept with her would mortify her. Just knowing we could smell her arousal and that she was going into heat had embarrassed her. I wanted to save her that pain.

And yet, I'd just traumatized her by yelling at her.

Bishop couldn't wake up fast enough. He was the only one who could patch up my complete fuck up, because it wasn't just me she was afraid of. I'd seen her shrink away from Deacon as well and suspected she was going to be that way with everyone until they proved to her she was safe.

Fuck.

I reached the top of the narrow stairs carved into the heart of the mountain that connected the Residence with the arena and opened the heavy wooden door. It opened into a hall in the storage area of the castle near the kitchens, and I took one of the many back staircases up to Bishop's suite.

Nova, I called out to her as I approached Bishop's door. There was a chance she wasn't in the Residence or even on the Residence's ground, and while I had the greatest telepathic reach in the pack, I still wouldn't be able to reach her if she were at the hospital.

Thankfully, as I opened Bishop's door, I felt her feathery mental touch indicating she'd heard me.

Where do you need me? she asked in her Nova-the-physician voice, which still, every time I heard it, surprised me. She'd been more mischievous than Deacon and Bishop combined when we were growing up.

Bishop's suite.

He hurt Bishop? she gasped, and I could just imagine the shock then deep worry flashing across her face before she was back in control of her emotions.

No. Knocked him out through their bond. I strode through Bishop's sitting room to his bedroom, past the clutter of finished and half finished paintings, painting supplies, and musical instruments.

What about you and Deacon?

A shift and a good night's sleep will suffice, I replied gruffly. I'd be exhausted for a couple of days but I'd be fine. I was more worried about Bishop. Knox had never knocked him out before and I was worried the mental blow had seriously hurt him.

The last time Bishop had pulled Knox back from the

brink of going completely feral, he'd been exhausted and had a headache for a week.

Of course, the last time, Knox's wolf hadn't been furious with me and Bishop. He'd ended up surrounded by a crowd with no easy way out and had panicked. This time, his wolf had taken over because we'd collared him. To protect Audrey.

I bit back a growl at how stupid I was as Nova hurried into Bishop's bedroom.

Knox's wolf had wanted Audrey from the start. Even feral, the chances he'd hurt her were slim.

Nova set her medical bag on the floor by her feet, sat on the bed beside Bishop, and went to work checking him over.

"His pulse is strong, his breathing normal," she said, pulling out a detection stone. It was mined near the underground lake where we got the water to make our elixirs and was imbued with some of the healing god's power as well. It didn't tell Nova what was wrong, but it did light up any area of the body that she needed to focus on. "Help me get him undressed."

"If there's nothing wrong," I said pulling Bishop into a sitting position so Nova could take off his shirt, "can you wake him?"

Because he needed to wake up and fix what I'd fucked up with Audrey. Yes, she needed to hate me, not flash me shy, heated looks that made both me and my wolf want to claim her, but she didn't have to be afraid of anyone else.

"I don't know if I can, but it would be best if we let

him wake naturally. I've never had a patient unconscious because of a soul bond."

Swell.

"Then after this, check on Deacon—"

Her eyes narrowed to the bloody mess I was still making of my pants and now Bishop's bed.

"Fine. Check me out after I shift, then Deacon, then check on Audrey. I might have—"

"Been yourself when it comes to women you're romantically interested in?" she asked in her driest possible tone.

"I'm not interested in her."

Her expression didn't change.

Yeah, I didn't believe myself, either.

AUDREY

I KNELT ON THE HARD ARENA FLOOR AND CRIED INTO MY hands, muffling my sobs, until I couldn't cry anymore. My eyes and throat hurt and my chest felt hollow like it had when Knox had rejected our bond.

A small voice inside me begged me to get up, do something, stand up for myself, but I had no idea what to do. I was permanently bound to Knox. I was trapped in Stonehaven and in this pack with no hope of escape until I died.

Was this how my father felt? Had he felt trapped in his nightmares? Had he known the only way to escape and end the horror was to die?

I didn't want to accept that killing myself was my only option, but there wasn't any other way to end my awful reality. I couldn't run away and there was no point in waiting for something to change. Nothing ever changed.

A part of me couldn't reconcile the Cyrus who'd just

yelled at me with the Cyrus who I'd walked with for a month. How could he have suddenly turned into an alpha like Merrick or Sterling?

No. He was worse than them. He'd hidden who he really was for our entire journey north and back. Sure, he hadn't been the most welcoming, but I hadn't thought he was a typical alpha. I'd thought we could have eventually become friends.

The memory of my fevered fantasy rushed through me and more tears threatened to fall.

I'd greedily fantasized that we could have been more than friends, even if I was mated to his brothers.

God, I was such an idiot. Such a stupid, foolish, naive little girl.

Even if I trusted that Bishop wasn't trying to trick me like Royce had, he wouldn't be able to protect me from Cyrus. Cyrus was the alpha. His word was pack law unless someone challenged him and won. But only a powerful alpha would be able to stand a chance against Cyrus and if I learned anything from this horrible lesson, it was that all alphas were the same.

Except Bishop was an alpha...

Which meant my nightmares had been right. He was using me and once he'd had his fun, I'd see the real Bishop just like I'd seen the real Cyrus.

I rasped a strangled sob, my eyes burning, too sore and dry to cry anymore.

It couldn't be true. That wasn't who Bishop was. That wasn't even who Cyrus really was. They were the men who'd made sure I ate when I was exhausted, who held me when I was tired, and who told me I had a future with their pack and with them. They weren't monsters like Merrick and Sterling and Royce.

But it didn't matter how much I wanted something to not be true. It didn't even matter if there was a chance it wasn't true. I couldn't let my guard down, couldn't be so stupidly trusting like I'd been for the last month. I had to stay quiet and stay small. For the rest of my life.

Which was no life at all.

Voices echoed in the vast arena, coming from the gated passage behind me, and I scrambled to my feet.

Stay quiet. Stay small.

Stay invisible.

Cyrus and Deacon had left on the far side of the arena where one of the gates was unlocked, and I bolted toward it. The voices behind me grew louder and the metal gate clanged open.

A masculine voice called out as I reached the passage and slipped into the darkness beyond. Thankfully, he didn't order me back and didn't release any alpha power to stop me, and I hurried down the passage into the wider hall.

The hall was still dimly lit and I prayed whoever was behind me wouldn't follow me. I probably shouldn't have fled and just faced whatever punishment they were going to give me. They were going to report what they'd seen to Cyrus, and he'd know I'd stayed where I wasn't supposed to be after he'd left.

But I hadn't been able to ignore the compulsion to flee. I was prey, after all, and running was what prey did.

The thought filled me with a bone deep exhaustion, and the small burst of energy that had propelled me out of the arena drained out of me, weighing me down.

Aimlessly, I followed the hall that turned out to be one large circle ringing the arena and returned to the large front entrance. Sunshine blazed in the courtyard beyond, an almost blinding light compared to the shadowy hall, but I didn't care. I wasn't sure if I cared about anything anymore.

If Cyrus wanted to find me, he'd find me. Once Knox woke, he'd be able to find me even faster since our mating bond was so strong I could feel when his emotions were raging out of control.

Despite that, I didn't want to go back to the Residence, didn't want to go back to the fancy suite. The door might not have been locked, but it was still a cage, and now I knew the truth. I was something to be toyed with until I was no longer entertaining, and I refused to be entertainment for an alpha ever again.

Which brought me back again to ending it all. It was the only thing left in my control.

My pulse lurched at the thought and my chest clenched as a voice within me, the one that wanted desperately to believe that being with Bishop hadn't been a lie and that gruff and distant Cyrus wasn't really a monster, begged me to reconsider.

There's another way. There's always another way. I'm just too tired to find it.

But my exhaustion and my grief were stronger, and I now knew the truth. That voice was just the last of my foolish hope, a hope that would have me continue to suffer.

Too tired to pay attention to where I was going, I stumbled into a narrow, shaded alley that reeked of rotting food and piss. At the end, sat a large wheeled bin with its lid hanging open and garbage spilling out. Someone had painted an uneven white circle on the bin's dented metal side and the ground in front of it was littered with broken bottles and ceramic jugs.

Guess even in this realm there were alleys like this. Not that I'd ever been to an alley like this in my realm. I'd only seen them on TV and the internet.

I turned to head back out onto the street, but the sight of the light at the end of the alley and the idea of taking another step was too much. I was exhausted just thinking about moving one more step. I just wanted to close my eyes and sleep.

Maybe when I woke this nightmare would be over.

I huffed to myself.

Who was I kidding? It would never be over and it didn't really matter where I stopped anyway.

I slid down the alley wall, hugged my knees to my chest, and closed my eyes. Staying here with the broken and discarded things was fitting for a broken and discarded shifter.

AUDREY

A DARK, MENACING LAUGH REVERBERATED AROUND ME AND someone screamed in agony. Merrick. Merrick was screaming. The monster was eating him alive and I was next.

Panic stole my breath and I ran. Tree branches clawed at my face and arms and tore into my dress more viciously in my dreams than they'd been in reality. Blood poured down my chest, stark against the shredded white fabric, while agony blazed through my body and my mind spun.

I had to get away. Had to—

The menacing laugh grew louder, a deep roiling sound with Merrick's screams a terrifying descant that made my soul tremble with fear.

"You can't escape," Sterling said, making me wrench my gaze around the dark forest, desperate to find him.

I was back in my old pack's sacred grove. Alone. My heart threatening to pound out of my chest.

With a lurch, I realized I was dreaming. Again. But that did little to ease the panic threatening to consume me.

"You're pathetic," Royce added. "So weak your only use is to be a sacrifice."

"No." I jerked around, trying to find them even though I knew I wouldn't until the dream wanted me to.

Were they behind me? I couldn't tell, couldn't see them, could barely see anything in the gloom.

The laugh roared through the glade, deafening me, making the trees and ground tremble, and stirring up a frozen wind that stung my skin.

"No one wants you," Sterling taunted.

"That's not true," I gasped. Bishop wanted me.

Except I didn't know that. Cyrus hadn't been who I'd thought he was. Bishop could be the same. My previous dreams could be right and everyone was just using me.

"You're a convenient cunt," Sterling laughed. "You begged for it and soon you'll go crawling back to them and beg some more."

"I won't," I insisted. I could be strong. But the second I thought that, I knew it wasn't true. I wasn't strong. I'd never be strong.

"Of course you will, because that's all that you're good for. Fuck toy or sacrifice." Sterling's laugh crescendoed, pressing in and oozing against my body as if it had physical mass even as the wind picked up and the trembling ground threaten to knock me over.

I tried to wipe the laugh away, but it clung to me, crawling over my skin and digging into the gashes Royce's claws had carved into my chest when he'd torn open my white transformation dress.

"I can't believe you were stupid enough to think I was your fated mate," Royce added, his voice suddenly right behind me.

I jerked around, my pulse roaring in my ears, bile burning my throat, but he wasn't there.

"Fate would never match me to someone like you," he hissed. "Fate wouldn't match you to anyone."

Not even to Bishop.

I knew that now. I'd seen the truth. I wasn't worthy.

But he'd promised—

And Royce had made me believe he'd wanted me, too.

I was so stupid. My throat tightened with tears. I'd fallen for the same trick in less than a month because I *was* desperate. Desperate for hope and love and all the things someone like me didn't deserve.

Except that doesn't make sense, a small voice whispered inside me, barely audible over Sterling's roaring laugh and stinging wind.

Of course, it didn't make sense. Nothing made sense. Because this was a dream.

Except even when I was awake my life didn't make sense. It never had.

"Because you're not supposed to be alive. You're

supposed to bleed," Sterling hissed, his voice coming from the right. "*He* desires your screams." No, Sterling was to my left.

I whirled around, jerking this way and that, but couldn't see anyone in the darkness and couldn't seem to make myself stop looking. If I had night vision like a normal shifter, I'd have been able to see him... maybe. No. I *would* have.

"Scream little wolf," Royce growled, his voice right behind me, making me lurch, my heart in my throat.

"No," I squeaked. "Never."

But I knew they could smell my fear, knew I'd finally come to realize that fighting them, fighting everything, was futile. It just prolonged my suffering.

"If you won't scream, then you'll bleed," Sterling snarled and dozens of flying snake monsters swarmed around me.

I batted my hands at the closest ones, slapping them away, but there were too many and they moved too quickly. Their sharp teeth tore into my flesh, while their tails wrapped around my arms, slowing my movement, and one wrapped around my throat, cutting off my air.

Another blast of laughter roared around me and the ground lurched beneath my feet. I heaved and squirmed, agony burning with every bite, each breath a desperate gasp. I had to get them off me, and I *had* to keep my balance. If I fell, I'd never get back up again.

"Scream, prey. Scream and cry and beg and feed Tzanagoth," Sterling howled, as the snake around my neck vanished and the agony in my body roared into an inferno, igniting every inch of me inside and out. "Scream and bleed."

"No," I forced out, tears streaming down my cheeks, as blood poured down my arms and chest. My white transformation dress was soaked and every time my blood splattered on the ground it exploded into a ball of red mist and birthed another snake.

I clawed and swatted at them, yanking one hand free, then the other only to be captured again. My heart pounded, threatening to tear out of my chest. I had to get them off me, had to run, had to escape.

But just as I heaved both arms free and wrenched away the snake around my neck and turned to flee, something seized my hair and jerked me back.

Royce.

He tightened his grip in my dirty blond locks, just like he had that horrible night, and he used it to haul me up until my bare toes skimmed the ground. Pain lanced through my scalp, and I heaved and clawed against his hold, uselessly repeating everything I'd tried the night of the transformation ceremony.

"You're supposed to scream," he snarled, raking his claws down my chest, ripping open my dress, and slicing into my flesh as if it hadn't just been ripped and bloody moments before.

I squeezed my eyes shut, praying I'd wake up.

It was just a dream. Just a dream.

"Waking won't be any better," Sterling laughed.

"You're still an alpha's whore and they're going to use you until you die."

They wouldn't. I wouldn't let them. Please. I couldn't.

But I was nothing compared to them, compared to everyone. They could take what they wanted and they would. They were alphas.

"No," I begged. "Please." Just the thought of seeing Bishop with Sterling or Royce's malicious expression hurt. He wasn't a psychopath. He couldn't be. He'd never use me like that... wouldn't he?

"Of course he won't," Royce growled. "I won't let him, because you're mine. You're my whore and I didn't get to fuck you."

Royce's black smoke lashed around my body, binding me to the ground, and the flying snakes latched onto me with their sharp teeth.

"You belong to me," he sneered as the snakes started burrowing into my skin.

Pain roared through me and I heaved against the smoke. They were going to take over, possess me. I could feel their sickening evil, born of violent blood sacrifices, oozing through my veins.

"No."

"Oh, yes," Sterling crowed.

"Please, no." I had to get free, had to get them off of me, out of me. I had to. I had to. They were going to take over, consume me from the inside out, and empower the malicious god that Sterling and Royce had tried to summon.

With a strength I didn't know I had, fueled by a panic that consumed all other thoughts, I wrenched one of my hands free and clawed at the snakes sinking into my skin.

"Get out. Get out!" I didn't belong to them. I didn't belong to anyone. Not even Knox. And I sure as hell wasn't going to let Tzanagoth consume me.

My hand hit a rock with a sharp edge and I seized it, slicing at the snakes trying to crawl under my skin. I'd kill them all. I wouldn't let them possess me. I wouldn't let anyone possess me, not Knox or Sterling or even a god.

I controlled my own fate no matter how lonely or pathetic it was.

Frantic, I slashed and swatted and fought. I freed my other hand and the smoky darkness tried to capture me again, but I writhed and twisted, avoiding its sticky grasp as more snakes tore at my skin.

Sterling stepped out of the grove, his eyes bright with a wicked smile, ghostly red rams horns curling from his temples like the depiction of Tzanagoth in Anakar. The terrifying power I'd sensed when he'd tried to get me to step into the rip and burn myself up, howled with the wind, suffocating and crushing, stronger than even Cyrus's alpha power.

"Yes," he cackled, his eyes bright with manic glee. "Bleed for me. Bleed!"

The snakes tore into my flesh and I screamed and screamed and—

— jerked awake.

Oh God.

It was a dream. Just a dream.

The reek of rotting food and piss hit my nose, then the metallic tang of blood. My head felt heavy, my body numb, even as my pulse pounded hard and fast.

I stood at the end of the alley, brandishing a broken bottle edged with blood, confused about how I'd gotten there and why I held the bottle.

Something plopped on my sandaled foot and I dragged my gaze, my thoughts working in slow motion, down down down my body.

Blood soaked my dress and rushed down my mutilated left arm. Everywhere there'd been a snake trying to possess me there were dozens of ragged slices, so many slices, so much blood, so—

Sterling's wicked laughter roared through me even though I was awake and the horror of what just happened stole my breath.

"Took you long enough," he taunted. "The sacrifice is now complete."

Don't miss the next book in the series!

Wolf Distressed

Ensnared by the Pack: Book Four

I've finally gotten a chance at happiness... but if it looks too good to be true, it probably is.

I'm the kind of girl who knows the other shoe is always going to drop. So now that something is going my way, that shoe should show up any minute now.

Knox and I have reached a tentative truce and things with Bishop have never been better. But no one in the pack trusts me and they sure don't trust me with their precious pack leaders. Especially the pack's favorite bachelor Bishop.

What's worse is Cyrus acting like my old alpha and me reacting like the old me. Fearful, afraid, feeling that gnawing instinct that tells me to run. And because it's Cyrus, his betrayal cuts deep. Deeper than I want to show.

Other than Bishop, I don't know who to trust, and if I can't find my way into the pack, to find a place here, then my future is set. And it's nothing good. I can't leave because I'm bound to Knox. I can't stay because I'm as welcome as mange.

Basically, I'm between a rock and a hard pack, and I'm afraid someone won't wait for Cyrus's permission and will send me packing... permanently.

OTHER BOOKS BY TESSA COLE

THE NEPHILIM'S DESTINY SERIES

Destined Shadows, prequel story

Destined Darkness, book 1

Destined Blood, book 2

Destined Fire, book 3

Destined Storm, book 4

Destined Radiance, book 5

THE ANGEL'S FATE SERIES

Fated Bonds, book 1

Fated Winter, book 2

Fated Fear, book 3

Fated Despair, book 4

Fated Resolve, book 5

Fated Heart, book 6

THE GRECIAN GODDESS TRILOGY

Kiss of the Goddess, book 1

Power of the Goddess, book 2

Bonds of the Goddess, book 3

ENSNARED BY THE PACK